Staffordshire Library and Information Service

Please return or renew by the last date shown

D1628542

PERIC

If not required by other readers, this item may be renewed
in person, by post or telephone, online or by email.
To renew, either the book or ticket are required

**24 Hour Renewal Line
0845 33 00 740**

Staffordshire
County Council

3 8014 05139 2287

The Perils of
Certain English Prisoners

Wilkie Collins and Charles Dickens

Edited by
Melisa Klimaszewski

Published by Hesperus Press Limited
28 Mortimer Street, London W1W 7RD
www.hesperuspress.com

First published in *Household Words* in 1857
First published by Hesperus Press Limited, 2012

This edition edited by Melisa Klimaszewski
Introduction, notes and note on the text © Melisa Klimaszewski, 2012

Designed and typeset by Fraser Muggeridge studio
Printed in Jordan by Jordan National Press

ISBN: 978-1-84391-389-4

CONTENTS

INTRODUCTION

This Christmas number is the only one of the eighteen that Dickens compiled to have a title mentioning Englishness. Clearly designed to evoke a protective feeling of solidarity with imperilled countrymen and women, the title is also tantalizingly vague. Which English prisoners are facing danger, and where in the world are they? With no location specified, readers might imagine India, where a violent rebellion against the English then called the 'Indian Mutiny' began on 10th May 1857, or the Crimea, where English soldiers had suffered many defeats in battles widely regarded to be managed poorly by military commanders. An average Victorian, then, may have been surprised to encounter a hybrid nautical/jungle adventure set in Central America in this issue's pages but probably would not have struggled to see the contemporary parallels. One review immediately identifies multiple symbolic counterparts, calling the number 'less a festive tribute to the season than a celebration of the great qualities displayed by our race in recent emergencies, Crimean and Indian'.[1]

Indeed, a robust assertion of Englishness as not just a national but a moral identity pervades the number, with others set in stark contrast to an exaggerated, and emphatically white, English purity. There is no avoiding the hatred that is targeted specifically at dark bodies in this story. From making a living 'table of black man's back', to casual references to 'niggers', to the villainous Pirate Captain's Portuguese 'brown fingers', this number shamelessly reiterates that threats to the most cherished of English ideals are spearheaded by corrupt people of colour who might not even be fully human. Even the 'English convicts' under the command of the Portuguese Pirate Captain seem to have been tainted more by 'the West India

Islands' than by their criminality, for they are singled out as the crew members who should have been murdering rather than obeying the Pirate Captain.

While the racism of the number's character portrayal is fairly straightforward, more complicated is the relationship of this story to Collins' and Dickens' personal views, particularly in regard to the Indian Rebellion. Multiple factors led to the violent agitation for Indian independence, but the trigger that began the bloodshed in 1857 concerned the greasing of ammunition cartridges (which had to be opened with one's teeth) with pig and cow fats. An Indian soldier, or sepoy, opening a cartridge was thereby forced to violate orthodox Muslim or Hindu beliefs. The British public was outraged that some women and children were killed in the insurrection, and military forces spent the next year reestablishing power at all costs, sometimes slaughtering entire Indian villages. Dickens explains in a letter to Henry Morley that his aim in this Christmas number is to 'shadow out' the bravery of the English, particularly the women, during this time of Rebellion.[2] 'Shadow', as anyone who has studied the endings of *Great Expectations* (1861) can attest, is a tricky term. A shadow is a form without detail, a shape that shifts, and a concept that suggests impermanence. In that context, this number does seem to capture shadows of both Collins' and Dickens' views of imperial perils.

The fact that Dickens' son Walter had just departed in July of 1857 for a post in India with the East India Company may have intensified Dickens' reaction to the Rebellion. In a letter to his friend Angela Burdett-Coutts, after stating that the unfair promotion of commissioned officers over non-commissioned ones makes him feel 'Demoniacal', Dickens continues,

And I wish I were Commander in Chief in India. The first thing I would do to strike that Oriental race with amazement (not in the least regarding them as if they lived in the Strand, London, or at Camden Town), should be to proclaim to them, in their language, that I considered my holding that appointment by the leave of God, to mean that I should do my utmost to exterminate the Race upon whom the stain of the late cruelties rested; and that I begged them to do me the favor to observe that I was there for that purpose and no other, and was now proceeding, with all convenient dispatch and merciful swiftness of execution, to blot it out of mankind and raze it off the face of the Earth.[3]

Many admirers of Dickens have found it difficult to reconcile such sentiments with their images of him as a benevolent man, and pondering the complexities of just this single paragraph – including questions of translation, space, and religion – certainly leads one to a more complicated view of an iconic writer. Although Dickens fantasizes about commanding a sort of divinely sanctioned genocide in this letter, and he puts nearly these exact words in Captain Carton's mouth (see page 24 below), the story in *The Perils* does not actually enact retributive violence on a massive scale. Critics disagree over the extent to which Collins' influence should be regarded as a factor that toned down Dickens' rage.

Collins was no stranger to racist character portrayals himself, and those wishing to identify Collins as less intensely racist must note that the only appearances of the word 'nigger' appear in Chapter Two, for which he is the primary author. His views on the Rebellion, however, do seem less extreme than Dickens' in that we do not have any record of Collins wishing to 'exterminate' a people. Collins' oeuvre also includes sympathetic representations of mixed race characters, and his 'Sermon for Sepoys', which appeared in *Household Words* on 27th February 1858, reminds readers of the long and respectable history of non-Christian religious beliefs, clearly working against mainstream depictions of Indians as ruthless savages.

Ultimately, *The Perils* is a collaborative work, only understood completely when all of its parts are considered together as a whole, and therefore attempting to understand the chapters as expressions of each individual writer's personal or political beliefs is likely to result in a skewed reading. The spirit of collaboration was high during the composition of this text, and Dickens and Collins conversed frequently enough for readers to conclude that the two men agreed on the direction of the number. They had collaborated on the previous year's Christmas number, *The Wreck of the Golden Mary*, and had also been working together on *The Frozen Deep*, a play they staged jointly in mostly private venues throughout 1857. For public performances of the play in Manchester, Ellen Ternan was one of the professional actresses who replaced Dickens' female relatives in the cast, and she became Dickens' love interest for the rest of his life.

Dickens and Collins found sustenance in their close friendship throughout this period as they collaborated regularly and faced enormous domestic changes. Dickens would split from his wife of more than twenty years to form a lifelong, secret liaison with Ternan. As Dickens was separating from Catherine, Collins was falling in love with the widowed Caroline Graves, acting as a father to her young daughter and sharing a home with her by the end of 1858. Excepting one brief separation, Collins lived with Graves for the rest of his life, but he never believed in the institution of marriage and later established a second home with Martha Rudd. At many of the pivotal moments in these relationships, Collins and Dickens were writing together.

In September of 1857, just a month after the conclusion of the Manchester *Frozen Deep* performances, the two took another trip northward to collect inspiration for *The Lazy Tour of Two Idle Apprentices* and to facilitate a Dickens/Ternan visit. A humorous collection of stories that feature Francis Goodchild and Thomas Idle, Dickens' and Collins' respective alter egos, *The Lazy Tour* shows the men light-heartedly fictionalising their relationship in the October pages of *Household Words*. They were clearly in sync creatively, and Collins was a paid staff writer, so it is not surprising that the two would collaborate again on that year's Christmas number. As with all of the Christmas numbers in his journal, Dickens' name was the only one to appear in print on the title page as the 'Conductor', and in his letters, he repeatedly tells friends that he wrote all but the second chapter. One may view such statements as Dickens claiming credit for a majority of the piece or as Dickens consistently insuring that Collins receives credit for the central chapter.

A Sotheby's catalogue for the sale of *The Perils* manuscript in 1890 includes 'the original sketch for the story, consisting of four pages, 8vo, by Wilkie Collins, and a long note by Dickens' and further describes 'a long letter from Collins to Dickens [...] discussing the Title and also giving many particulars of the proposed plot'. These documents do not appear to have survived with the other Collins manuscripts sold in the auction lot, but there is no reason to doubt the accuracy of the catalogue, and its descriptions contradict critical appraisals of this number that presume Dickens to be a bullying creative force rather than an engaged collaborator.

Especially to a reader who is not familiar with each author's individual works, without the headings designating authorship, it is easy to read the number and hear one authorial voice. Each man was a strong author in his own right, and each was willing to position himself narratively as an illiterate man forced to place the story into the hands of a more educated woman. The narrative voice does not shift radically for the middle section, nor does the tone or style vary so profoundly as to cause confusion. The pacing of the second chapter is rapid, consistent with many of Collins' novels, but the suspenseful events of that portion also coincide with the moments when readers would naturally expect to find the plot's climax. The themes that one encounters – innocent children, cross-class romantic desire, imperial violence, heroic women, inventive escapes – arise in future works by both Collins and Dickens. Captain Carton's name famously reappears in Dickens' *A Tale of Two Cities* (1859), and the heroine of Collins' phenomenally popular *The Woman in White* (1859–60) is another Marian. Dickens' *Great Expectations* (1860–1) features a working-class man pining for a woman who has been raised to regard herself as his social superior, and *The Moonstone* (1868) shows Collins continuing to question the moral soundness of British imperial wealth acquired in India. We will never know how much the social time Collins and Dickens shared, or the personal jokes they enjoyed as confidants, influenced each writer's individual publications, but their frequent collaborations and the apparent cross-pollination of themes suggest a persistent conversation amongst their works.

A present-day reader might be surprised that the special Christmas issue of Dickens' journal does not mention Christmas directly or illustrate that holiday's celebrations. An eccentric pirate with scented handkerchiefs, or a heroine who knows her way around a pile of broadswords and muskets, may not sound like typical Christmas fare, but Dickens was pleased with this number's emotional arc. Despite his nationalistic goals, it was not the treachery of the pirates or the bravery of their English victims that moved him most intensely, but rather Gill Davis' affection for Marion Maryon. In a dramatic letter to Lady Duff Gordon, Dickens explains that overwhelming sentiment kept him from being able to face the proof pages until the very last moment: 'It was only when the Steam Engine roared for the sheets, that I could find it in my heart to look at them with a pen in my hand dipped in any thing but tears!'[4] Fortunately, Dickens did manage to correct the proofs with actual ink, putting the finishing touches on a Christmas number that continues to reach an eager audience.

– *Melisa Klimaszewski, 2012*

NOTE ON THE TEXT

The Perils of Certain English Prisoners was originally published on 7th December 1857 as a special issue or number of *Household Words*, the weekly journal that Charles Dickens founded in 1850 and for which he served as chief editor. The original publication did not identify Wilkie Collins as a co-writer, stating only that the number was 'Conducted by Charles Dickens'. This edition identifies the portion for which Wilkie Collins is the main author.

Attribution is a difficult practice in regard to any collaborative text. For *The Perils*, a Sotheby's catalogue lists the manuscript for sale at an 1890 auction along with other Collins manuscripts, and its whereabouts, if it survives, are not presently known. It is impossible to determine the level of influence Collins and Dickens had on one another's prose or the degree to which they discussed and agreed upon textual details during the great amount of time they spent together. We also do not know the extent to which Dickens revised the entire text at the galley proof stage before it appeared in *Household Words*, the pages of which he edited meticulously each week.

The Sotheby's catalogue describes 'the original sketch for the story' in Collins' hand, a letter from Collins to Dickens with plot details, and corrections throughout in both men's hands. Therefore, it is prudent for readers to keep in mind that the text as a whole is a collaboration even though the surviving correspondence of Collins and Dickens, Collins' notations on the manuscript, and subsequent reprintings of portions of the text under a single author's name make it possible to say with confidence that Dickens is the primary author of Chapters I and III while Collins is the primary author of Chapter II.

In 1858, an authorized collection titled *Novels and Tales Reprinted from Household Words* (Volume 7), published in Germany by Bernhard Tauchnitz, included the full text of *The Perils* with only Dickens identified as Conductor. Chapman and Hall issued a one-volume edition of the *Household Words* Christmas numbers in 1859 that included the full text of *The Perils* with no attribution of Chapter II to Collins, and future collections of the *Household Words* numbers continued that practice. An 1890 Chapman and Hall edition of *The Lazy Tour of Two Idle Apprentices and Other Stories* included *The Perils* as well as *No Thoroughfare* with both Collins and Dickens identified as authors on the title page.

In 1867, Dickens selected some of his own stories from several of the *Household Words* Christmas numbers for republication but did not include *The Perils*. After his death, the Charles Dickens Edition of his works included only Chapter I and Chapter III of *The Perils*, an editorial choice repeated in the 1898 Gadshill Edition of Dickens' oeuvre and other later collections. The Everyman edition of *The Christmas Stories*, edited by Ruth Glancy and published in 1996, prints *The Perils* in its entirety with Collins identified as the second chapter's author.

My editorial practices preserve the text's original punctuation and capitalisation with a minimum of modernisation. I have retained inconsistent capitalisation because Dickens and his colleagues so often used capitalisation for emphasis or for other intentional reasons. Except in cases of obvious printer errors, or instances where an apparent error obscures meaning, I have retained the text's original punctuation, which includes what may seem like excessive commas to today's readers and semi-colons where today's practices would call for commas. Nineteenth-century spellings (such as 'chace') and usages (such as 'eat' instead of 'ate') have been retained, but inconsistencies within the text (such as appearances of 'honour' as well as 'honor') have been made consistent with present-day usage. The most standardisation appears in regard to hyphens. I have modernised hyphenated as well as compound words (such as to-morrow, cocoa-nut, and sea shore) that are now understood as single words, and I follow Oxford's guidelines regarding compound words that take hyphens when attributive.

These practices are consistent with other collaborative Dickens works now in print from Hesperus.

The Perils of
Certain English Prisoners

and Their Treasure in
Women, Children, Silver, and Jewels

THE EXTRA CHRISTMAS NUMBER OF
HOUSEHOLD WORDS

CONDUCTED BY CHARLES DICKENS

CONTAINING THE AMOUNT OF
ONE NUMBER AND A HALF

CHRISTMAS, 1857

CHAPTER I
THE ISLAND OF SILVER-STORE
[by Charles Dickens]

It was in the year of our Lord one thousand seven hundred and forty-four, that I, Gill Davis to command, His Mark,[5] having then the honour to be a private in the Royal Marines, stood a-leaning over the bulwarks of the armed sloop Christopher Columbus, in the South American waters off the Mosquito shore.[6]

My lady remarks to me, before I go any further, that there is no such Christian name as Gill, and that her confident opinion is, that the name given to me in the baptism wherein I was made, &c., was Gilbert. She is certain to be right, but I never heard of it. I was a foundling child, picked up somewhere or another, and I always understood my Christian name to be Gill. It is true that I was called Gills when employed at Snorridge Bottom[7] betwixt Chatham and Maidstone to frighten birds; but that had nothing to do with the Baptism wherein I was made, &c., and wherein a number of things were promised for me by somebody, who let me alone ever afterwards as to performing any of them, and who, I consider, must have been the Beadle.[8] Such name of Gills was entirely owing to my cheeks, or gills, which at that time of my life were of a raspy description.

My lady stops me again, before I go any further, by laughing exactly in her old way and waving the feather of her pen at me. That action on her part, calls to my mind as I look at her hand with the rings on it – Well! I won't! To be sure it will come in, in its own place. But it's always strange to me, noticing the quiet hand, and noticing it (as I have done, you know, so many times) a-fondling children and grandchildren asleep, to think that when blood and honour were up – there! I won't! not at present! – Scratch it out.

She won't scratch it out, and quite honourable; because we have made an understanding that everything is to be taken down, and that nothing that is once taken down shall be scratched out. I have the great misfortune not to be able to read and write, and I am speaking my true and faithful account of those Adventures, and my lady is writing it, word for word.

I say, there I was, a-leaning over the bulwarks of the sloop Christopher Columbus in the South American waters off the Mosquito shore: a subject of his Gracious Majesty King George of England, and a private in the Royal Marines.

In those climates, you don't want to do much. I was doing nothing. I was thinking of the shepherd (my father, I wonder?) on the hillsides by Snorridge Bottom, with a long staff, and with a rough white coat in all weathers all the year round,[9] who used to let me lie in a corner of his hut by night, and who used to let me go about with him and his sheep by day when I could get nothing else to do, and who used to give me so little of his victuals and so much of his staff, that I ran away from him – which was what he wanted all along, I expect – to be knocked about the world in preference to Snorridge Bottom. I had been knocked about the world for nine-and-twenty years in all, when I stood looking along those bright blue South American waters. Looking after the shepherd, I may say. Watching him in a half-waking dream, with my eyes half-shut, as he, and his flock of sheep, and his two dogs, seemed to move away from the ship's side, far away over the blue water, and go right down into the sky.

'It's rising out of the water, steady,' a voice said close to me. I had been thinking on so, that it like woke me with a start, though it was no stranger voice than the voice of Harry Charker, my own comrade.

'What's rising out of the water, steady?' I asked my comrade.

'What?' says he. 'The Island.'

'O! The Island!' says I, turning my eyes towards it. 'True. I forgot the Island.'

'Forgot the port you're going to? That's odd, an't it?'

'It is odd,' says I.

'And odd,' he said, slowly considering with himself, 'an't even. Is it, Gill?'

He had always a remark just like that to make, and seldom another. As soon as he had brought a thing round to what it was not, he was satisfied. He was one of the best of men, and, in a certain sort of a way, one with the least to say for himself. I qualify it, because, besides being able to read and write like a quartermaster,[10] he had always one most excellent idea in his mind. That was, Duty. Upon my soul, I don't believe, though I admire learning beyond everything, that he could have got a better idea out of all the books in the world, if he had learnt them every word, and been the cleverest of scholars.

My comrade and I had been quartered in Jamaica, and from there we had been drafted off to the British settlement of Belize, lying away West and North of the Mosquito coast.[11] At Belize there had been great alarm of one cruel gang of pirates (there were always more pirates than enough in those Caribbean Seas), and as they got the better of our English cruisers by running into out-of-the-way creeks and shallows, and taking the land when they were hotly pressed, the governor of Belize had received orders from home to keep a sharp lookout for them along shore. Now, there was an armed sloop came once a year from Port Royal, Jamaica, to the Island, laden with all manner of necessaries, to eat and to drink, and to wear, and to use in various ways; and it was aboard of that sloop which had touched at Belize, that I was a-standing, leaning over the bulwarks.

The Island was occupied by a very small English colony. It had been given the name of Silver-Store. The reason of its being so called, was, that the English colony owned and worked a silver mine over on the mainland, in Honduras, and used this island as a safe and convenient place to store their silver in, until it was annually fetched away by the sloop. It was brought down from the mine to the coast on the backs of mules, attended by friendly Indians and guarded by white men; from thence, it was conveyed over to Silver-Store, when the weather was fair, in the canoes of that country; from Silver-Store, it was carried to Jamaica by the armed sloop once a year, as I have already mentioned; from Jamaica, it went, of course, all over the world.

How I came to be aboard the armed sloop, is easily told. Four-and-twenty marines under command of a lieutenant – that officer's name was Linderwood – had been told off at Belize, to proceed to Silver-Store, in aid of boats and seamen stationed there for the chace of the Pirates. The island was considered a good post of observation against the pirates, both by land and sea; neither the pirate ship nor yet her boats had been seen by any of us, but they had been so much heard of, that the reinforcement was sent. Of that party, I was one. It included a corporal and a serjeant. Charker was corporal, and the serjeant's name was Drooce. He was the most tyrannical non-commissioned officer[12] in His Majesty's service.

The night came on, soon after I had had the foregoing words with Charker. All the wonderful bright colors went out of the sea and sky, in a few minutes, and all the stars in the

Heavens seemed to shine out together, and to look down at themselves in the sea, over one another's shoulders, millions deep. Next morning, we cast anchor off the Island. There was a snug harbor within a little reef; there was a sandy beach; there were coconut trees with high straight stems, quite bare, and foliage at the top like plumes of magnificent green feathers; there were all the objects that are usually seen in those parts, and I am not going to describe them, having something else to tell about.

Great rejoicings, to be sure, were made on our arrival. All the flags in the place were hoisted, all the guns in the place were fired, and all the people in the place came down to look at us. One of those Sambo fellows – they call those natives Sambos, when they are half-negro and half-Indian[13] – had come off outside the reef, to pilot us in, and remained on board after we had let go our anchor. He was called Christian George King, and was fonder of all hands than anybody else was. Now, I confess, for myself, that on that first day, if I had been captain of the Christopher Columbus, instead of private in the Royal Marines, I should have kicked Christian George King – who was no more a Christian, than he was a King, or a George – over the side, without exactly knowing why, except that it was the right thing to do.

But, I must likewise confess, that I was not in a particularly pleasant humor, when I stood under arms that morning, aboard the Christopher Columbus in the harbor of the Island of Silver-Store. I had had a hard life, and the life of the English on the Island seemed too easy and too gay, to please me. 'Here you are,' I thought to myself, 'good scholars and good livers; able to read what you like, able to write what you like, able to eat and drink what you like, and spend what you like, and do what you like; and much *you* care for a poor, ignorant

7

Private in the Royal Marines! Yet it's hard, too, I think, that you should have all the halfpence, and I all the kicks; you all the smooth, and I all the rough; you all the oil, and I all the vinegar.' It was as envious a thing to think as might be, let alone its being nonsensical; but, I thought it. I took it so much amiss, that, when a very beautiful young English lady came aboard, I grunted to myself, 'Ah! *you* have got a lover, I'll be bound!' As if there was any new offence to me in that, if she had!

She was sister to the captain of our sloop, who had been in a poor way for some time, and who was so ill then that he was obliged to be carried ashore. She was the child of a military officer, and had come out there with her sister, who was married to one of the owners of the silver mine, and who had three children with her. It was easy to see that she was the light and spirit of the Island. After I had got a good look at her, I grunted to myself again, in an even worse state of mind than before, 'I'll be damned, if I don't hate him, whoever he is!'

My officer, Lieutenant Linderwood, was as ill as the captain of the sloop, and was carried ashore, too. They were both young men of about my age, who had been delicate in the West India climate. I even took *that*, in bad part. I thought I was much fitter for the work than they were, and that if all of us had our deserts, I should be both of them rolled into one. (It may be imagined what sort of an officer of marines I should have made, without the power of reading a written order. And as to any knowledge how to command the sloop – Lord! I should have sunk her in a quarter of an hour!)

However, such were my reflections; and when we men were ashore and dismissed, I strolled about the place along with Charker, making my observations in a similar spirit.

It was a pretty place: in all its arrangements partly South American and partly English, and very agreeable to look at on that account, being like a bit of home that had got chipped off and had floated away to that spot, accommodating itself to circumstances as it drifted along. The huts of the Sambos, to the number of five-and-twenty, perhaps, were down by the beach to the left of the anchorage. On the right was a sort of barrack, with a South American Flag[14] and the Union Jack, flying from the same staff, where the little English colony could all come together, if they saw occasion. It was a walled square of building, with a sort of pleasure ground inside, and inside that again a sunken block like a powder magazine, with a little square trench round it, and steps down to the door. Charker and I were looking in at the gate, which was not guarded; and I had said to Charker, in reference to the bit like a powder magazine, 'that's where they keep the silver, you see;' and Charker had said to me, after thinking it over, 'And silver an't gold. Is it, Gill?' when the beautiful young English lady I had been so bilious about, looked out of a door, or a window – at all events looked out, from under a bright awning. She no sooner saw us two in uniform, than she came out so quickly that she was still putting on her broad Mexican hat of plaited straw when we saluted.

'Would you like to come in,' she said, 'and see the place? It is rather a curious place.'

We thanked the young lady, and said we didn't wish to be troublesome; but, she said it could be no trouble to an English soldier's daughter, to show English soldiers how their countrymen and countrywomen fared, so far away from England; and consequently we saluted again, and went in. Then, as we stood in the shade, she showed us (being as affable as beautiful), how the different families lived in their separate houses, and how there was a general house for stores, and a general reading room, and a general room for music and dancing, and a room for Church; and how there were other houses on the rising ground called the Signal Hill, where they lived in the hotter weather.

'Your officer has been carried up there,' she said, 'and my brother, too, for the better air. At present, our few residents are dispersed over both spots: deducting, that is to say, such of our number as are always going to, or coming from, or staying at, the Mine.'

('*He* is among one of those parties,' I thought, 'and I wish somebody would knock his head off.')

'Some of our married ladies live here,' she said, 'during at least half the year, as lonely as widows, with their children.'

'Many children here, ma'am?'

'Seventeen. There are thirteen married ladies, and there are eight like me.'

There were not eight like her – there was not one like her – in the world. She meant, single.

'Which, with about thirty Englishmen of various degrees,' said the young lady, 'form the little colony now on the Island. I don't count the sailors, for they don't belong to us. Nor the soldiers,' she gave us a gracious smile when she spoke of the soldiers, 'for the same reason.'

'Nor the Sambos, ma'am,' said I.

'No.'

'Under your favor, and with your leave, ma'am,' said I, 'are they trustworthy?'

'Perfectly! We are all very kind to them, and they are very grateful to us.'

'Indeed, ma'am? Now – Christian George King? –'

'Very much attached to us all. Would die for us.'

She was, as in my uneducated way I have observed very beautiful women almost always to be, so composed, that her composure gave great weight to what she said, and I believed it.

Then, she pointed out to us the building like a powder magazine, and explained to us in what manner the silver was brought from the mine, and was brought over from the mainland, and was stored there. The Christopher Columbus would have a rich lading, she said, for there had been a great yield that year, a much richer yield than usual, and there was a chest of jewels besides the silver.

When we had looked about us, and were getting sheepish, through fearing we were troublesome, she turned us over to a young woman, English born but West India bred, who served her as her maid. This young woman was the widow of a non-commissioned officer in a regiment of the line. She had got married and widowed at St Vincent,[15] with only a few months between the two events. She was a little saucy woman, with a bright pair of eyes, rather a neat little foot and figure, and rather a neat little turned-up nose. The sort of young woman, I considered at the time, who appeared to invite you to give her a kiss, and who would have slapped your face if you accepted the invitation.

I couldn't make out her name at first; for, when she gave it in answer to my inquiry, it sounded like Beltot, which didn't sound right. But, when we became better acquainted – which was while Charker and I were drinking sugar-cane sangaree,[16] which she made in a most excellent manner – I found that her Christian name was Isabella, which they shortened into Bell, and that the name of the deceased non-commissioned officer was Tott. Being the kind of neat little woman it was natural to make a toy of, – I never saw a woman so like a toy in my life – she had got the plaything name of Belltott. In short, she had no other name on the island. Even Mr Commissioner

Pordage[17] (and *he* was a grave one!) formally addressed her as Mrs Belltott. But, I shall come to Mr Commissioner Pordage presently.

The name of the captain of the sloop was Captain Maryon, and therefore it was no news to hear from Mrs Belltott, that his sister, the beautiful unmarried young English lady, was Miss Maryon. The novelty was, that her Christian name was Marion too. Marion Maryon. Many a time I have run off those two names in my thoughts, like a bit of verse. O many, and many, and many, a time!

We saw out all the drink that was produced, like good men and true, and then took our leaves, and went down to the beach. The weather was beautiful; the wind steady, low, and gentle; the island, a picture; the sea, a picture; the sky, a picture. In that country there are two rainy seasons in the year. One sets in at about our English Midsummer; the other, about a fortnight after our English Michaelmas.[18] It was the beginning of August at that time; the first of these rainy seasons was well over; and everything was in its most beautiful growth, and had its loveliest look upon it.

'They enjoy themselves here,' I says to Charker, turning surly again. 'This is better than private soldiering.'

We had come down to the beach, to be friendly with the boat's crew who were camped and hutted there; and we were approaching towards their quarters over the sand, when Christian George King comes up from the landing place at a wolf's-trot, crying, 'Yup, So-Jeer!' – which was that Sambo Pilot's barbarous way of saying, Hallo, Soldier! I have stated myself to be a man of no learning, and, if I entertain prejudices, I hope allowance may be made. I will now confess to one. It may be a right one or it may be a wrong one; but, I never did like Natives, except in the form of oysters.[19]

So, when Christian George King, who was individually unpleasant to me besides, comes a trotting along the sand, clucking 'Yup, So-Jeer!' I had a thundering good mind to let fly at him with my right. I certainly should have done it, but that it would have exposed me to reprimand.

'Yup, So-Jeer!' says he. 'Bad job.'

'What do you mean?' says I.

'Yup, So-Jeer!' says he, 'Ship Leakee.'

'Ship leaky?' says I.

'Iss,' says he, with a nod that looked as if it was jerked out of him by a most violent hiccup – which is the way with those savages.

I cast my eyes at Charker, and we both heard the pumps going aboard the sloop, and saw the signal run up, 'Come on board; hands wanted from the shore.' In no time some of the sloop's liberty-men[20] were already running down to the water's edge, and the party of seamen, under orders against the Pirates, were putting off to the Columbus in two boats.

'Oh Christian George King sar berry sorry!' says that Sambo vagabond, then. 'Christian George King cry, English fashion!' His English fashion of crying was to screw his black knuckles into his eyes, howl like a dog, and roll himself on his back on the sand. It was trying not to kick him, but I gave Charker the word, 'Double-quick, Harry!' and we got down to the water's edge, and got on board the sloop.

By some means or other, she had sprung such a leak, that no pumping would keep her free; and what between the two fears that she would go down in the harbor, and that, even if she did not, all the supplies she had brought for the little colony would be destroyed by the seawater as it rose in her, there was great confusion. In the midst of it, Captain Maryon was heard hailing from the beach. He had been carried down in his hammock, and looked very bad; but, he insisted on being stood there on his feet; and I saw him, myself, come off in the boat, sitting upright in the stern sheets,[21] as if nothing was wrong with him.

A quick sort of council was held, and Captain Maryon soon resolved that we must all fall to work to get the cargo out, and, that when that was done, the guns and heavy matters must be got out, and that the sloop must be hauled ashore, and careened, and the leak stopped. We were all mustered (the Pirate-Chace party volunteering), and told off into parties, with so many hours of spell and so many hours of relief, and we all went at it with a will. Christian George King was entered one of the party in which I worked, at his own request, and he went at it with as good a will as any of the rest. He went at it with so much heartiness, to say the truth, that he rose in my good opinion, almost as fast as the water rose in the ship. Which was fast enough, and faster.

Mr Commissioner Pordage kept in a red and black japanned[22] box, like a family lump-sugar box, some document or other which some Sambo chief or other had got drunk and spilt some ink over (as well as I could understand the matter), and by that means had given up lawful possession of the Island. Through having hold of this box, Mr Pordage got his title of Commissioner. He was styled Consul, too, and spoke of himself as 'Government'.

He was a stiff-jointed, high-nosed old gentleman, without an ounce of fat on him, of a very angry temper and a very yellow complexion. Mrs Commissioner Pordage, making allowance for difference of sex, was much the same. Mr Kitten, a small, youngish, bald, botanical and mineralogical gentleman, also connected with the mine – but everybody there was that, more or less – was sometimes called by Mr Commissioner Pordage, his Vice Commissioner, and sometimes his Deputy-consul. Or sometimes he spoke of Mr Kitten, merely as being 'under Government'.

The beach was beginning to be a lively scene with the preparations for careening the sloop, and, with cargo, and spars, and rigging, and water casks, dotted about it, and with temporary quarters for the men rising up there out of such sails and odds and ends as could be best set on one side to make them, when Mr Commissioner Pordage comes down in a high fluster, and asks for Captain Maryon. The Captain, ill as he was, was slung in his hammock betwixt two trees, that he might direct; and he raised his head, and answered for himself.

'Captain Maryon,' cries Mr Commissioner Pordage, 'this is not official. This is not regular.'

'Sir,' says the Captain, 'it hath been arranged with the clerk and supercargo, that you should be communicated with, and requested to render any little assistance that may lie in your power. I am quite certain that hath been duly done.'

'Captain Maryon,' replies Mr Commissioner Pordage, 'there hath been no written correspondence. No documents have passed, no memoranda have been made, no minutes have been made, no entries and counter-entries appear in the official muniments. This is indecent. I call upon you, sir, to desist, until all is regular, or Government will take this up.'

'Sir,' says Captain Maryon, chafing a little, as he looked out of his hammock; 'between the chances of Government taking this up, and my ship taking herself down, I much prefer to trust myself to the former.'

'You do, sir?' cries Mr Commissioner Pordage.

'I do, sir,' says Captain Maryon, lying down again.

'Then, Mr Kitten,' says the Commissioner, 'send up instantly for my Diplomatic coat.'

He was dressed in a linen suit at that moment; but, Mr Kitten started off himself and brought down the Diplomatic coat, which was a blue cloth one, gold-laced, and with a crown on the button.

'Now, Mr Kitten,' says Pordage, 'I instruct you, as Vice Commissioner, and Deputy-consul of this place, to demand of Captain Maryon, of the sloop Christopher Columbus, whether he drives me to the act of putting this coat on?'

'Mr Pordage,' says Captain Maryon, looking out of his hammock again, 'as I can hear what you say, I can answer it without troubling the gentleman. I should be sorry that you should be at the pains of putting on too hot a coat on my account; but, otherwise, you may put it on hind side before, or inside out, or with your legs in the sleeves, or your head in the skirts, for any objection that I have to offer to your thoroughly pleasing yourself.'

'Very good, Captain Maryon,' says Pordage, in a tremendous passion. 'Very good, sir. Be the consequences on your own head! Mr Kitten, as it has come to this, help me on with it.'

When he had given that order, he walked off in the coat, and all our names were taken, and I was afterwards told that Mr Kitten wrote from his dictation more than a bushel of large paper on the subject, which cost more before it was done with, than ever could be calculated, and which only got done with after all, by being lost.

Our work went on merrily, nevertheless, and the Christopher Columbus, hauled up, lay helpless on her side like a great fish out of water. While she was in that state, there was a feast, or a ball, or an entertainment, or more properly all three together, given us in honour of the ship, and the ship's company, and the other visitors. At that assembly, I believe, I saw all the inhabitants then upon the Island, without any exception. I took no particular notice of more than a few, but I found it very agreeable in that little corner of the world to see the children, who were of all ages, and mostly very pretty – as they mostly are. There was one handsome elderly lady, with very dark eyes and grey hair, that I inquired about. I was told that her name was Mrs Venning; and her married daughter, a fair slight thing, was pointed out to me by the name of Fanny Fisher. Quite a child she looked, with a little copy of herself holding to her dress; and her husband, just come back from the mine, exceeding proud of her. They were a good-looking set of people on the whole, but I didn't like them. I was out of sorts; in conversation with Charker, I found fault with all of them. I said of Mrs Venning, she was proud; of Mrs Fisher, she was a delicate little baby-fool. What did I think of this one? Why, he was a fine gentleman. What did I say to that one? Why, she was a fine lady. What could you expect them to be (I asked Charker), nursed in that climate, with the tropical night shining for them, musical instruments playing to them, great trees bending over them, soft lamps lighting them, fireflies sparkling in among them, bright flowers and birds brought into existence to please their eyes, delicious drinks to be had for the pouring out, delicious fruits to be got for the picking, and every one dancing and murmuring happily in the scented air, with the sea breaking low on the reef for a pleasant chorus.

'Fine gentlemen and fine ladies, Harry?' I says to Charker. 'Yes, I think so! Dolls! Dolls! Not the sort of stuff for wear, that comes of poor private soldiering in the Royal Marines!'

However, I could not gainsay that they were very hospitable people, and that they treated us uncommonly well. Every man of us was at the entertainment, and Mrs Belltott had more partners than she could dance with: though she danced all night, too. As to Jack (whether of the Christopher Columbus, or of the Pirate pursuit party, it made no difference), he danced with his brother Jack, danced with himself, danced with the moon, the stars, the trees, the prospect, anything. I didn't greatly take to the chief officer of that party, with his bright eyes, brown face, and easy figure. I didn't much like his way when he first happened to come where we were, with Miss Maryon on his arm. 'Oh, Captain Carton,' she says, 'here are two friends of mine!' He says, 'Indeed? These two Marines?' – meaning Charker and self. 'Yes,' says she, 'I showed these two friends of mine when they first came, all the wonders of Silver-Store.' He gave us a laughing look, and says he, 'You are in luck, men. I would be disrated and go before the mast tomorrow, to be shown the way upward again by such a guide. You are in luck, men.' When we had saluted, and he and the young lady had waltzed away, I said, 'You are a pretty fellow, too, to talk of luck. You may go to the Devil!'

Mr Commissioner Pordage and Mrs Commissioner, showed among the company on that occasion like the King and Queen of a much Greater Britain than Great Britain. Only two other circumstances in that jovial night made much separate impression on me. One was this. A man in our draft of marines, named Tom Packer, a wild unsteady young fellow, but the son of a respectable shipwright in Portsmouth Yard, and a good scholar who had been well brought up, comes to me after a spell of dancing, and takes me aside by the elbow, and says, swearing angrily:

'Gill Davis, I hope I may not be the death of Serjeant Drooce one day!'

Now, I knew Drooce always had borne particularly hard on this man, and I knew this man to be of a very hot temper: so, I said:

'Tut, nonsense! don't talk so to me! If there's a man in the corps who scorns the name of an assassin, that man and Tom Packer are one.'

Tom wipes his head, being in a mortal sweat, and says he:

'I hope so, but I can't answer for myself when he lords it over me, as he has just now done, before a woman. I tell you what, Gill! Mark my words! It will go hard with Serjeant Drooce, if ever we are in an engagement together, and he has to look to me to save him. Let him say a prayer then, if he knows one, for it's all over with him, and he is on his Deathbed. Mark my words!'

I did mark his words, and very soon afterwards, too, as will shortly be taken down.

The other circumstance that I noticed at that ball, was, the gaiety and attachment of Christian George King. The innocent spirits that Sambo Pilot was in, and the impossibility he found himself under of showing all the little colony, but especially the ladies and children, how fond he was of them, how devoted to them, and how faithful to them for life and death, for present, future, and everlasting, made a great impression on me. If ever a man, Sambo or no Sambo, was trustful and trusted, to what may be called quite an infantine and sweetly beautiful extent, surely, I thought that morning when I did at last lie down to rest, it was that Sambo Pilot, Christian George King.

This may account for my dreaming of him. He stuck in my sleep, cornerwise, and I couldn't get him out. He was always flitting about me, dancing round me, and peeping in over my hammock, though I woke and dozed off again fifty times. At last, when I opened my eyes, there he really was, looking in at the open side of the little dark hut; which was made of leaves, and had Charker's hammock slung in it as well as mine.

'So-Jeer!' says he, in a sort of a low croak. 'Yup!'

'Hallo!' says I, starting up. 'What? You *are* there, are you?'

'Iss,' says he. 'Christian George King got news.'

'What news has he got?'

'Pirates out!'

I was on my feet in a second. So was Charker. We were both aware that Captain Carton, in command of the boats, constantly watched the mainland for a secret signal, though, of course, it was not known to such as us what the signal was.

Christian George King had vanished before we touched the ground. But, the word was already passing from hut to hut to turn out quietly, and we knew that the nimble barbarian had got hold of the truth, or something near it.

In a space among the trees behind the encampment of us visitors, naval and military, was a snugly-screened spot, where we kept the stores that were in use, and did our cookery. The word was passed to assemble here. It was very quickly given, and was given (so far as we were concerned) by Serjeant Drooce, who was as good in a soldier point of view, as he was bad in a tyrannical one. We were ordered to drop into this space, quietly, behind the trees, one by one. As we assembled here, the seamen assembled too. Within ten minutes, as I should estimate, we were all here, except the usual guard upon the beach. The beach (we could see it through the wood) looked as it always had done in the hottest time of the day. The guard were in the shadow of the sloop's hull, and nothing was moving but the sea, and that moved very faintly. Work had always been knocked off at that hour, until the sun grew less fierce, and the sea breeze rose; so that its being holiday with us, made no difference, just then, in the look of the place. But, I may mention that it was a holiday, and the first we had had since our hard work began. Last night's ball had been given, on the leak's being repaired, and the careening done. The worst of the work was over, and tomorrow we were to begin to get the sloop afloat again.

We marines were now drawn up here, under arms. The chace-party were drawn up separate. The men of the Columbus were drawn up separate. The officers stepped out into the midst of the three parties, and spoke so as all might hear. Captain Carton was the officer in command, and he had a spyglass in his hand. His coxswain[23] stood by him with another spyglass, and with a slate on which he seemed to have been taking down signals.

'Now, men!' says Captain Carton; 'I have to let you know, for your satisfaction: Firstly, that there are ten pirate boats, strongly-manned and armed, lying hidden up a creek yonder on the coast, under the overhanging branches of the dense trees. Secondly, that they will certainly come out this night when the moon rises, on a pillaging and murdering expedition, of which some part of the mainland is the object. Thirdly – don't cheer, men! – that we will give chace, and, if we can get at them, rid the world of them, please God!'

Nobody spoke, that I heard, and nobody moved, that I saw. Yet there was a kind of ring, as if every man answered and approved with the best blood that was inside of him.

'Sir,' says Captain Maryon, 'I beg to volunteer on this service, with my boats. My people volunteer, to the ship's boys.'

'In His Majesty's name and service,' the other answers, touching his hat, 'I accept your aid with pleasure. Lieutenant Linderwood, how will you divide your men?'

I was ashamed – I give it out to be written down as large and plain as possible – I was heart and soul ashamed of my thoughts of those two sick officers, Captain Maryon and Lieutenant Linderwood, when I saw them, then and there. The spirit in those two gentlemen beat down their illness (and very ill I knew them to be) like Saint George beating down the Dragon.[24] Pain and weakness, want of ease and want of rest, had no more place in their minds than fear itself. Meaning now to express for my lady to write down, exactly what I felt then and there, I felt this: 'You two brave fellows that I have been so grudgeful of, I know that if you were dying you would put it off to get up and do your best, and then you would be so modest that in lying down again to die, you would hardly say, "I did it!"'

It did me good. It really did me good.

But, to go back to where I broke off. Says Captain Carton to Lieutenant Linderwood, 'Sir, how will you divide your men? There is not room for all; and a few men should, in any case, be left here.'

There was some debate about it. At last, it was resolved to leave eight Marines and four seamen on the Island, besides the sloop's two boys. And because it was considered that the friendly Sambos would only want to be commanded in case of any danger (though none at all was apprehended there), the officers were in favour of leaving the two non-commissioned officers, Drooce and Charker. It was a heavy disappointment to them, just as my being one of the left was a heavy disappointment to me – then, but not soon afterwards. We men drew lots for it, and I drew 'Island'. So did Tom Packer. So, of course, did four more of our rank and file.

When this was settled, verbal instructions were given to all hands to keep the intended expedition secret, in order that the women and children might not be alarmed, or the expedition put in a difficulty by more volunteers. The assembly was to be on that same spot at sunset. Every man was to keep up an appearance, meanwhile, of occupying himself in his usual way. That is to say, every man excepting four old trusty seamen, who were appointed, with an officer, to see to the arms and ammunition, and to muffle the rullocks[25] of the boats, and to make everything as trim and swift and silent as it could be made.

The Sambo Pilot had been present all the while, in case of his being wanted, and had said to the officer in command, five hundred times over if he had said it once, that Christian George King would stay with the So-Jeers, and take care of the booffer ladies and the booffer childs – booffer being that native's expression for beautiful. He was now asked a few questions concerning the putting off of the boats, and in particular whether there was any way of embarking at the back of the Island: which Captain Carton would have half liked to do, and then have dropped round in its shadow and slanted across to the main. But, 'No,' says Christian George King. 'No, no, no! Told you so, ten time. No, no, no! All reef, all rock, all swim, all drown!' Striking out as he said it, like a swimmer gone mad, and turning over on his back on dry land, and spluttering himself to death, in a manner that made him quite an exhibition.

The sun went down, after appearing to be a long time about it, and the assembly was called. Every man answered to his name, of course, and was at his post. It was not yet black dark, and the roll was only just gone through, when up comes Mr Commissioner Pordage with his Diplomatic coat on.

'Captain Carton,' says he, 'Sir, what is this?'

'This, Mr Commissioner,' (he was very short with him) 'is an expedition against the Pirates. It is a secret expedition, so please to keep it a secret.'

'Sir,' says Commissioner Pordage, 'I trust there is going to be no unnecessary cruelty committed?'

'Sir,' returns the officer, 'I trust not.'

'That is not enough, sir,' cries Commissioner Pordage, getting wroth. 'Captain Carton, I give you notice. Government requires you to treat the enemy with great delicacy, consideration, clemency, and forbearance.'

'Sir,' says Captain Carton, 'I am an English Officer, commanding English Men, and I hope I am not likely to disappoint the Government's just expectations. But, I presume you know that these villains under their black flag[26] have despoiled our countrymen of their property, burnt their homes, barbarously murdered them and their little children, and worse than murdered their wives and daughters?'

'Perhaps I do, Captain Carton,' answers Pordage, waving his hand, with dignity; 'perhaps I do not. It is not customary, sir, for Government to commit itself.'

'It matters very little, Mr Pordage, whether or no. Believing that, I hold my commission by the allowance of God, and not that I have received it direct from the Devil, I shall certainly use it, with all avoidance of unnecessary suffering and with all merciful swiftness of execution, to exterminate these people from the face of the earth.[27] Let me recommend you to go home, sir, and to keep out of the night air.'

Never another syllable did that officer say to the Commissioner, but turned away to his men. The Commissioner buttoned his Diplomatic coat to the chin, said, 'Mr Kitten, attend me!' gasped, half choked himself, and took himself off.

It now fell very dark, indeed. I have seldom, if ever, seen it darker, nor yet so dark. The moon was not due until one in the morning, and it was but a little after nine when our men lay down where they were mustered. It was pretended that they were to take a nap, but everybody knew that no nap was to be got under the circumstances. Though all were very quiet, there was a restlessness among the people; much what I have seen among the people on a racecourse, when the bell has rung for the saddling for a great race with large stakes on it.

At ten, they put off; only one boat putting off at a time; another following in five minutes; both then lying on their oars until another followed. Ahead of all, paddling his own outlandish little canoe without a sound, went the Sambo pilot, to take them safely outside the reef. No light was shown but once, and that was in the commanding officer's own hand. I lighted the dark lantern for him, and he took it from me when he embarked. They had blue lights and such like with them, but kept themselves as dark as Murder.

The expedition got away with wonderful quietness, and Christian George King soon came back, dancing with joy.

'Yup, So-Jeer,' says he to myself in a very objectionable kind of convulsions, 'Christian George King sar berry glad. Pirates all be blown a-pieces. Yup! Yup!'

My reply to that cannibal was, 'However glad you may be, hold your noise, and don't dance jigs and slap your knees about it, for I can't abear to see you do it.'

I was on duty then; we twelve who were left, being divided into four watches of three each, three hours' spell. I was relieved at twelve. A little before that time, I had challenged, and Miss Maryon and Mrs Belltott had come in.

'Good Davis,' says Miss Maryon, 'what is the matter? Where is my brother?'

I told her what was the matter, and where her brother was.

'O Heaven help him!' says she, clasping her hands and looking up – she was close in front of me, and she looked most lovely to be sure; 'he is not sufficiently recovered, not strong enough for such strife!'

'If you had seen him, miss,' I told her, 'as I saw him when he volunteered, you would have known that his spirit is strong enough for any strife. It will bear his body, miss, to wherever duty calls him. It will always bear him to an honourable life, or a brave death.'

'Heaven bless you!' says she, touching my arm. 'I know it. Heaven bless you!'

Mrs Belltott surprised me by trembling and saying nothing. They were still standing looking towards the sea and listening, after the relief had come round. It continuing very dark, I asked to be allowed to take them back. Miss Maryon thanked me, and she put her arm in mine, and I did take them back. I have now got to make a confession that will appear singular. After I had left them, I laid myself down on my face on the beach, and cried, for the first time since I had frightened birds as a boy at Snorridge Bottom, to think what a poor, ignorant, low-placed, private soldier I was.

It was only for half a minute or so. A man can't at all times be quite master of himself, and it was only for half a minute or so. Then I up and went to my hut, and turned into my hammock, and fell asleep with wet eyelashes, and a sore, sore heart. Just as I had often done when I was a child, and had been worse used than usual.

I slept (as a child under those circumstances might) very sound, and yet very sore at heart all through my sleep. I was awoke by the words, 'He is a determined man.' I had sprung out of my hammock, and had seized my firelock, and was standing on the ground, saying the words myself. 'He is a determined man.' But, the curiosity of my state was, that I seemed to be repeating them after somebody, and to have been wonderfully startled by hearing them.

As soon as I came to myself, I went out of the hut, and away to where the guard was. Charker challenged: 'Who goes there?'

'A friend.'

'Not Gill?' says he, as he shouldered his piece.

'Gill,' says I.

'Why, what the deuce do you do out of your hammock?' says he.

'Too hot for sleep,' says I; 'is all right?'

'Right!' says Charker, 'yes, yes; all's right enough here; what should be wrong here? It's the boats that we want to know of. Except for fireflies twinkling about, and the lonesome splashes of great creatures as they drop into the water, there's nothing going on here to ease a man's mind from the boats.'

The moon was above the sea, and had risen, I should say, some half an hour. As Charker spoke, with his face towards the sea, I, looking landward, suddenly laid my right hand on his breast, and said, 'Don't move. Don't turn. Don't raise your voice! You never saw a Maltese face[28] here?'

'No. What do you mean?' he asks, staring at me.

'Nor yet an English face, with one eye and a patch across the nose?'

'No. What ails you? What do you mean?'

I had seen both, looking at us round the stem of a coconut tree, where the moon struck them. I had seen that Sambo Pilot, with one hand laid on the stem of the tree, drawing them back into the heavy shadow. I had seen their naked cutlasses twinkle and shine, like bits of the moonshine in the water that had got blown ashore among the trees by the light wind. I had seen it all, in a moment. And I saw in a moment (as any man would), that the signalled move of the pirates on the mainland was a plot and a feint; that the leak had been made to disable the sloop; that the boats had been tempted away, to leave the Island unprotected; that the pirates had landed by some secreted way at the back; and that Christian George King was a double-dyed traitor,[29] and a most infernal villain.

I considered, still all in one and the same moment, that Charker was a brave man, but not quick with his head; and that Serjeant Drooce, with a much better head, was close by. All I said to Charker was, 'I am afraid we are betrayed. Turn your back full to the moonlight on the sea, and cover the stem of the coconut tree which will then be right before you, at the height of a man's heart. Are you right?'

'I am right,' says Charker, turning instantly, and falling into the position with a nerve of iron; 'and right a'nt left. Is it Gill?'

A few seconds brought me to Serjeant Drooce's hut. He was fast asleep, and being a heavy sleeper, I had to lay my hand upon him to rouse him. The instant I touched him he came rolling out of his hammock, and upon me like a tiger. And a tiger he was, except that he knew what he was up to, in his utmost heat, as well as any man.

I had to struggle with him pretty hard to bring him to his senses, panting all the while (for he gave me a breather[30]), 'Serjeant, I am Gill Davis! Treachery! Pirates on the Island!'

The last words brought him round, and he took his hands off. 'I have seen two of them within this minute,' said I. And so I told him what I had told Harry Charker.

His soldierly, though tyrannical, head was clear in an instant. He didn't waste one word, even of surprise. 'Order the guard,' says he, 'to draw off quietly into the Fort.' (They called the enclosure I have before mentioned, the Fort, though it was not much of that.) 'Then get you to the Fort as quick as you can, rouse up every soul there, and fasten the gate. I will bring in all those who are up at the Signal Hill. If we are surrounded before we can join you, you must make a sally and cut us out if you can. The word among our men is, "Women and children!"'

He burst away, like fire going before the wind over dry reeds. He roused up the seven men who were off duty, and had them bursting away with him, before they knew they were not asleep. I reported orders to Charker, and ran to the Fort, as I have never run at any other time in all my life: no, not even in a dream.

The gate was not fast, and had no good fastening: only a double wooden bar, a poor chain, and a bad lock. Those, I secured as well as they could be secured in a few seconds by one pair of hands, and so ran to that part of the building where Miss Maryon lived. I called to her loudly by her name until she answered. I then called loudly all the names I knew – Mrs Macey (Miss Maryon's married sister), Mr Macey, Mrs Venning, Mr and Mrs Fisher, even Mr and Mrs Pordage. Then I called out, 'All you gentlemen here, get up and defend the place! We are caught in a trap. Pirates have landed. We are attacked!'

At the terrible word 'Pirates!' – for, those villains had done such deeds in those seas as never can be told in writing, and can scarcely be so much as thought of – cries and screams rose up from every part of the place. Quickly, lights moved about from window to window, and the cries moved about with them, and men, women and children came flying down into the square. I remarked to myself, even then, what a number of things I seemed to see at once. I noticed Mrs Macey coming towards me, carrying all her three children together. I noticed Mr Pordage, in the greatest terror, in vain trying to get on his Diplomatic coat; and Mr Kitten respectfully tying his pocket handkerchief over Mrs Pordage's nightcap. I noticed Mrs Belltott run out screaming, and shrink upon the ground near me, and cover her face in her hands, and lie, all of a bundle, shivering. But, what I noticed with the greatest pleasure was, the determined eyes with which those men of the Mine that I had thought fine gentlemen, came round me with what arms they had: to the full as cool and resolute as I could be, for my life – aye, and for my soul, too, into the bargain!

The chief person being Mr Macey, I told him how the three men of the guard would be at the gate directly, if they were not already there, and how Serjeant Drooce and the other seven were gone to bring in the outlying part of the people of Silver-Store. I next urged him, for the love of all who were dear to him, to trust no Sambo, and, above all, if he could get any good chance at Christian George King, not to lose it, but to put him out of the world. 'I will follow your advice to the letter, Davis,' says he; 'what next?'

My answer was, 'I think, sir, I would recommend you next, to order down such heavy furniture and lumber as can be moved, and make a barricade within the gate.'

'That's good again,' says he; 'will you see it done?'

'I'll willingly help to do it,' says I, 'unless or until my superior, Serjeant Drooce, gives me other orders.'

He shook me by the hand, and having told off some of his companions to help me, bestirred himself to look to the arms and ammunition. A proper quick, brave, steady, ready gentleman!

One of their three little children was deaf and dumb. Miss Maryon had been from the first with all the children, soothing them, and dressing them (poor little things, they had been brought out of their beds), and making them believe that it was a game of play, so that some of them were now even laughing. I had been working hard with the others at the barricade, and had got up a pretty good breastwork within the gate. Drooce and the seven men had come back, bringing in the people from the Signal Hill, and had worked along with us: but, I had not so much as spoken a word to Drooce, nor had Drooce so much as spoken a word to me, for we were both too busy. The breastwork was now finished, and I found Miss Maryon at my side, with a child in her arms. Her dark hair was fastened round her head with a band. She had a quantity of it, and it looked even richer and more precious, put up hastily out of her way, than I had seen it look when it was carefully arranged. She was very pale, but extraordinarily quiet and still.

'Dear good Davis,' said she, 'I have been waiting to speak one word to you.'

I turned to her directly. If I had received a musketball in the heart, and she had stood there, I almost believe I should have turned to her before I dropped.

'This pretty little creature,' said she, kissing the child in her arms, who was playing with her hair and trying to pull it down, 'cannot hear what we say – can hear nothing. I trust you so much, and have such great confidence in you, that I want you to make me a promise.'

'What is it, Miss?'

'That if we are defeated, and you are absolutely sure of my being taken, you will kill me.'

'I shall not be alive to do it, Miss. I shall have died in your defence before it comes to that. They must step across my body, to lay a hand on you.'

'But, if you are alive, you brave soldier.' How she looked at me! 'And if you cannot save me from the Pirates, living, you will save me, dead. Tell me so.'

Well! I told her I would do that, at the last, if all else failed. She took my hand – my rough, coarse hand – and put it to her lips. She put it to the child's lips, and the child kissed it. I believe I had the strength of half a dozen men in me, from that moment, until the fight was over.

All this time, Mr Commissioner Pordage had been wanting to make a Proclamation to the Pirates, to lay down their arms and go away; and everybody had been hustling him about and tumbling over him, while he was calling for pen and ink to write it with. Mrs Pordage, too, had some curious ideas about the British respectability of her nightcap (which had as many frills to it, growing in layers one inside another, as if it was a white vegetable of the artichoke sort), and she wouldn't take the nightcap off, and would be angry when it got crushed by the other ladies who were handing things about, and, in short, she gave as much trouble as her husband did. But, as we were now forming for the defence of the place, they were both poked out of the way with no ceremony. The children and ladies were got into the little trench which surrounded the silver-house (we were afraid of leaving them in any of the light buildings, lest they should be set on fire), and we made the best disposition we could. There was a pretty good store, in point of amount, of tolerable swords and cutlasses.[31] Those were issued. There were, also, perhaps a score or so of spare muskets. Those were brought out. To my astonishment, little Mrs Fisher that I had taken for a doll and a baby, was not only very active in that service, but volunteered to load the spare arms.

'For, I understand it well,' says she, cheerfully, without a shake in her voice.

'I am a soldier's daughter and a sailor's sister, and I understand it too,' says Miss Maryon, just in the same way.

Steady and busy behind where I stood, those two beautiful and delicate young women fell to handling the guns, hammering the flints, looking to the locks, and quietly directing others to pass up powder and bullets from hand to hand, as unflinching as the best of tried soldiers.

Serjeant Drooce had brought in word that the pirates were very strong in numbers – over a hundred, was his estimate –

and that they were not, even then, all landed; for, he had seen them in a very good position on the further side of the Signal Hill, evidently waiting for the rest of their men to come up. In the present pause, the first we had had since the alarm, he was telling this over again to Mr Macey, when Mr Macey suddenly cried out:

'The signal! Nobody has thought of the signal!'

We knew of no signal, so we could not have thought of it. 'What signal may you mean, sir?' says Serjeant Drooce, looking sharp at him.

'There is a pile of wood upon the Signal Hill. If it could be lighted – which never has been done yet – it would be a signal of distress to the mainland.'

Charker cries, directly: 'Serjeant Drooce, dispatch me on that duty. Give me the two men who were on guard with me tonight, and I'll light the fire, if it can be done.'

'And if it can't, Corporal –' Mr Macey strikes in.

'Look at these ladies and children, sir!' says Charker. 'I'd sooner *light myself*, than not try any chance to save them.'

We gave him a Hurrah! – it burst from us, come of it what might – and he got his two men, and was let out at the gate, and crept away. I had no sooner come back to my place from being one of the party to handle the gate, than Miss Maryon said in a low voice behind me:

'Davis, will you look at this powder. This is not right?'

I turned my head. Christian George King again, and treachery again! Seawater had been conveyed into the magazine, and every grain of powder was spoiled!

'Stay a moment,' said Serjeant Drooce, when I had told him, without causing a movement in a muscle of his face: 'look to your pouch, my lad. You Tom Packer, look to your pouch, confound you! Look to your pouches, all you Marines.'

The same artful savage had got at them, somehow or another, and the cartridges were all unserviceable. 'Hum!' says the Serjeant, 'Look to your loading, men. You are right so far?'

Yes; we were right so far.

'Well, my lads, and gentlemen all,' says the Serjeant, 'this will be a hand-to-hand affair, and so much the better.'

He treated himself to a pinch of snuff, and stood up, square-shouldered and broad-chested, in the light of the moon – which was now very bright – as cool as if he was waiting for a play to begin. He stood quiet, and we all stood quiet, for a matter of something like half an hour. I took notice from such whispered talk as there was, how little we that the silver did not belong to, thought about it, and how much the people that it did belong to, thought about it. At the end of the half-hour, it was reported from the gate that Charker and the two were falling back on us, pursued by about a dozen.

'Sally! Gate-party, under Gill Davis,' says the Serjeant, 'and bring 'em in! Like men, now!'

We were not long about it, and we brought them in. 'Don't take me,' says Charker, holding me round the neck, and stumbling down at my feet when the gate was fast, 'don't take me near the ladies or the children, Gill. They had better not see Death, till it can't be helped. They'll see it soon enough.'

'Harry!' I answered, holding up his head. 'Comrade!'

He was cut to pieces. The signal had been secured by the first pirate party that landed; his hair was all singed off, and his face was blackened with the running pitch from a torch.

He made no complaint of pain, or of anything. 'Good bye, old chap,' was all he said, with a smile. 'I've got my death. And Death a'nt life. Is it, Gill?'

Having helped to lay his poor body on one side, I went back to my post. Serjeant Drooce looked at me, with his eyebrows a little lifted. I nodded. 'Close up here, men, and gentlemen all!' said the Serjeant. 'A place too many, in the line.'

The Pirates were so close upon us at this time, that the foremost of them were already before the gate. More and more came up with a great noise, and shouting loudly. When we believed from the sound that they were all there, we gave three English cheers. The poor little children joined, and were so fully convinced of our being at play, that they enjoyed the noise, and were heard clapping their hands in the silence that followed.

Our disposition was this, beginning with the rear. Mrs Venning, holding her daughter's child in her arms, sat on the steps of the little square trench surrounding the silver-house, encouraging and directing those women and children as she might have done in the happiest and easiest time of her life. Then, there was an armed line, under Mr Macey, across the width of the enclosure, facing that way and having their backs towards the gate, in order that they might watch the walls and prevent our being taken by surprise. Then, there was a space of eight or ten feet deep, in which the spare arms were, and in which Miss Maryon and Mrs Fisher, their hands and dresses blackened with the spoilt gunpowder, worked on their knees, tying such things as knives, old bayonets, and spearheads, to the muzzles of the useless muskets. Then, there was a second armed line, under Serjeant Drooce, also across the width of the enclosure, but facing to the gate. Then, came the breastwork we had made, with a zigzag way through it for me and my little party to hold good in retreating, as long as we could, when we were driven from the gate. We all knew that it was impossible to hold the place long, and that our only hope was in the timely discovery of the plot by the boats, and in their coming back.

I and my men were now thrown forward to the gate. From a spyhole, I could see the whole crowd of Pirates. There were Malays among them, Dutch, Maltese, Greeks, Sambos, Negroes, and Convict Englishmen from the West India Islands; among the last, him with the one eye and the patch across the nose. There were some Portuguese, too, and a few Spaniards. The captain was a Portuguese; a little man with very large earrings under a very broad hat, and a great bright shawl twisted about his shoulders. They were all strongly armed, but like a boarding party, with pikes, swords, cutlasses, and axes. I noticed a good many pistols, but not a gun of any kind among them. This gave me to understand that they had considered that a continued roll of musketry might perhaps have been heard on the mainland; also, that for the reason that fire would be seen from the mainland they would not set the Fort in flames and roast us alive; which was one of their favorite ways of carrying on. I looked about for Christian George King, and if I had seen him I am much mistaken if he would not have received my one round of ball-cartridge in his head. But, no Christian George King was visible.

A sort of a wild Portuguese demon, who seemed either fierce-mad or fierce-drunk – but, they all seemed one or the other – came forward with the black flag, and gave it a wave or two. After that, the Portuguese captain called out in shrill English, 'I say you! English fools! Open the gate! Surrender!'

As we kept close and quiet, he said something to his men which I didn't understand, and when he had said it, the one-eyed English rascal with the patch (who had stepped out when he began), said it again in English. It was only this. 'Boys of the black flag, this is to be quickly done. Take all the prisoners you can. If they don't yield, kill the children to make them. Forward!' Then, they all came on at the gate, and, in another half minute were smashing and splitting it in.

We struck at them through the gaps and shivers, and we dropped many of them, too; but, their very weight would have carried such a gate, if they had been unarmed. I soon found Serjeant Drooce at my side, forming us six remaining marines in line – Tom Packer next to me – and ordering us to fall back three paces, and, as they broke in, to give them our one little volley at short distance. 'Then,' says he, 'receive them behind your breastwork on the bayonet, and at least let every man of you pin one of the cursed cockchafers[32] through the body.'

We checked them by our fire, slight as it was, and we checked them at the breastwork. However, they broke over it like swarms of devils – they were, really and truly, more devils than men – and then it was hand to hand, indeed.

We clubbed our muskets and laid about us; even then, those two ladies – always behind me – were steady and ready with the arms. I had a lot of Maltese and Malays upon me, and, but for a broadsword that Miss Maryon's own hand put in mine, should have got my end from them. But, was that all? No. I saw a heap of banded dark hair and a white dress come thrice between me and them, under my own raised right arm, which each time might have destroyed the wearer of the white dress; and each time one of the lot went down, struck dead.

Drooce was armed with a broadsword, too, and did such things with it, that there was a cry, in half a dozen languages, of 'Kill that serjeant!' as I knew, by the cry being raised in English, and taken up in other tongues. I had received a severe cut across the left arm a few moments before, and should have known nothing of it, except supposing that somebody had struck me a smart blow, if I had not felt weak, and seen myself covered with spouting blood, and, at the same instant of time, seen Miss Maryon tearing her dress, and binding it with Mrs Fisher's help round the wound. They called to Tom Packer, who was scouring by, to stop and guard me for one minute, while I was bound, or I should bleed to death in trying to defend myself. Tom stopped directly, with a good sabre in his hand.

In that same moment – all things seem to happen in that same moment, at such a time – half a dozen had rushed howling at Serjeant Drooce. The Serjeant, stepping back against the wall, stopped one howl forever with such a terrible blow, and waited for the rest to come on, with such a wonderfully unmoved face, that they stopped and looked at him.

'See him now!' cried Tom Packer. 'Now, when I could cut him out! Gill! Did I tell you to mark my words?'

I implored Tom Packer in the Lord's name, as well as I could in my faintness, to go to the Serjeant's aid.

'I hate and detest him,' says Tom, moodily wavering. 'Still, he is a brave man.' Then he calls out, 'Serjeant Drooce, Serjeant Drooce! Tell me you have driven me too hard, and are sorry for it.'

The Serjeant, without turning his eyes from his assailants, which would have been instant death to him, answers:

'No. I won't.'

'Serjeant Drooce!' cries Tom, in a kind of an agony. 'I have passed my word that I would never save you from Death, if I could, but would leave you to die. Tell me you have driven me too hard and are sorry for it, and that shall go for nothing.'

One of the group laid the Serjeant's bald bare head open. The Serjeant laid him dead.

'I tell you,' says the Serjeant, breathing a little short, and waiting for the next attack. 'No. I won't. If you are not man enough to strike for a fellow soldier because he wants help, and because of nothing else, I'll go into the other world and look for a better man.'

Tom swept upon them, and cut him out. Tom and he fought their way through another knot of them, and sent them flying, and came over to where I was beginning again to feel, with inexpressible joy, that I had got a sword in my hand.

They had hardly come to us, when I heard, above all the other noises, a tremendous cry of women's voices. I also saw Miss Maryon, with quite a new face, suddenly clap her two hands over Mrs Fisher's eyes. I looked towards the silver-house, and saw Mrs Venning – standing upright on the top of the steps of the trench, with her grey hair and her dark eyes – hide her daughter's child behind her, among the folds of her dress, strike a pirate with her other hand, and fall, shot by his pistol.

The cry arose again, and there was a terrible and confusing rush of the women into the midst of the struggle. In another moment, something came tumbling down upon me that I thought was the wall. It was a heap of Sambos who had come over the wall; and of four men who clung to my legs like serpents, one who clung to my right leg was Christian George King.

'Yup, So-Jeer!' says he, 'Christian George King sar berry glad So-Jeer a prisoner. Christian George King been waiting for So-Jeer sech long time. Yup, yup!'

What could I do, with five-and-twenty of them on me, but be tied hand and foot? So, I was tied hand and foot. It was all over now – boats not come back – all lost! When I was fast bound and was put up against the wall, the one-eyed English convict came up with the Portuguese Captain, to have a look at me.

'See!' says he, 'Here's the determined man! If you had slept sounder, last night, you'd have slept your soundest last night, my determined man.'

The Portuguese Captain laughed in a cool way, and, with the flat of his cutlass, hit me crosswise, as if I was the bough of a tree that he played with: first on the face, and then across the chest and the wounded arm. I looked him steady in the face without tumbling while he looked at me, I am happy to say; but, when they went away, I fell, and lay there.

The sun was up, when I was roused and told to come down to the beach and be embarked. I was full of aches and pains, and could not at first remember; but, I remembered quite soon enough. The killed were lying about all over the place, and the Pirates were burying their dead, and taking away their wounded on hastily-made litters, to the back of the Island. As for us prisoners, some of their boats had come round to the usual harbor, to carry us off. We looked a wretched few, I thought, when I got down there; still, it was another sign that we had fought well, and made the enemy suffer.

The Portuguese Captain had all the women already embarked in the boat he himself commanded, which was just putting off when I got down. Miss Maryon sat on one side of him, and gave me a moment's look, as full of quiet courage, and pity, and confidence, as if it had been an hour long. On the other side of him was poor little Mrs Fisher, weeping for her child and her mother. I was shoved into the same boat with Drooce and Packer, and the remainder of our party of marines: of whom we had lost two privates, besides Charker, my poor, brave comrade. We all made a melancholy passage, under the hot sun, over to the mainland. There, we landed in a solitary place, and were mustered on the sea sand. Mr and Mrs Macey and their children were amongst us, Mr and Mrs Pordage, Mr Kitten, Mr Fisher, and Mrs Belltott. We mustered only fourteen men, fifteen women, and seven children. Those were all that remained of the English who had lain down to sleep last night, unsuspecting and happy, on the Island of Silver-Store.

CHAPTER II
THE PRISON IN THE WOODS
[by Wilkie Collins]

There we all stood, huddled up on the beach under the burning sun, with the pirates closing us in on every side – as forlorn a company of helpless men, women, and children as ever was gathered together out of any nation in the world. I kept my thoughts to myself; but I did not in my heart believe that any one of our lives was worth five minutes' purchase.

The man on whose will our safety or our destruction depended was the Pirate Captain. All our eyes, by a kind of instinct, fixed themselves on him – excepting in the case of the poor children, who, too frightened to cry, stood hiding their faces against their mothers' gowns. The ruler who held all the ruffians about us in subjection, was, judging by appearances, the very last man I should have picked out as likely to fill a place of power among any body of men, good or bad, under heaven. By nation, he was a Portuguese; and, by name, he was generally spoken of among his men as The Don. He was a little, active, weazen,[33] monkey-faced man, dressed in the brightest colours and the finest made clothes I ever saw. His three-cornered hat was smartly cocked on one side. His coat-skirts were stiffened and stuck out, like the skirts of the dandies in the Mall in London.[34] When the dance was given at the Island, I saw no such lace on any lady's dress there as I saw on his cravat and ruffles. Round his neck he wore a thick gold chain, with a diamond cross hanging from it. His lean, wiry, brown fingers were covered with rings. Over his shoulders, and falling down in front to below his waist, he wore a sort of sling of broad scarlet cloth, embroidered with beads and little feathers, and holding, at the lower part, four loaded pistols, two on a side, lying ready to either hand. His face was mere skin and bone, and one of his wrinkled cheeks had a blue scar running all across it, which drew up that part of his face, and showed his white shining teeth on that side of his mouth. An uglier, meaner, weaker, man-monkey to look at, I never saw; and yet there was not one of his crew, from his mate to his cabin boy, who did not obey him as if he had been the greatest monarch in the world. As for the Sambos, including especially that evil-minded scoundrel, Christian George King, they never went near him without seeming to want to roll before him on the ground, for the sake of winning the honour of having one of his little dancing master's feet set on their black bullock bodies.[35]

There this fellow stood, while we were looking at him, with his hands in his pockets, smoking a cigar. His mate (the one-eyed Englishman), stood by him; a big, hulking fellow he was, who might have eaten the Captain up, pistols and all, and looked about for more afterwards. The Don himself seemed, to an ignorant man like me, to have a gift of speaking in any tongue he liked. I can testify that his English rattled out of his crooked lips as fast as if it was natural to them; making allowance, of course, for his foreign way of clipping his words.

'Now, Captain,' says the big mate, running his eye over us as if we were a herd of cattle, 'here they are. What's to be done with them?'

'Are they all off the Island?' says the Pirate Captain.

'All of them that are alive,' says the mate.

'Good, and very good,' says the captain. 'Now, Giant-Georgy, some paper, a pen, and a horn of ink.'

Those things were brought immediately.

'Something to write on,' says the Pirate Captain. 'What? Ha! why not a broad nigger back?'

He pointed with the end of his cigar to one of the Sambos. The man was pulled forward, and set down on his knees with his shoulders rounded. The Pirate Captain laid the paper on them, and took a dip of ink – then suddenly turned up his snub nose with a look of disgust, and, removing the paper again, took from his pocket a fine cambric[36] handkerchief edged with lace, smelt at the scent on it, and afterwards laid it delicately over the Sambo's shoulders.

'A table of black man's back, with the sun on it, close under my nose – ah, Giant-Georgy, pah! pah!' says the Pirate Captain, putting the paper on the handkerchief, with another grimace expressive of great disgust.

He began to write immediately, waiting from time to time to consider a little with himself; and once stopping, apparently, to count our numbers as we stood before him. To think of that villain knowing how to write, and of my not being able to make so much as a decent pothook,[37] if it had been to save my life!

When he had done, he signed to one of his men to take the scented handkerchief off the Sambo's back, and told the sailor he might keep it for his trouble. Then, holding the written paper open in his hand, he came forward a step or two closer to us, and said, with a grin, and a mock bow, which made my fingers itch with wanting to be at him:

'I have the honour of addressing myself to the ladies. According to my reckoning they are fifteen ladies in all. Does any one of them belong to the chief officer of the sloop?'

There was a momentary silence.

'You don't answer me,' says the Pirate Captain. 'Now, I mean to be answered. Look here, women.' He drew one of his four pistols out of his gay scarlet sling, and walked up to Tom Packer, who happened to be standing nearest to him of the men prisoners. 'This is a pistol, and it is loaded. I put the barrel to the head of this man with my right hand, and I take out my watch with my left. I wait five minutes for an answer. If I don't get it in five minutes, I blow this man's brains out. I wait five minutes again, and if I don't get an answer, I blow the next man's brains out. And so I go on, if you are obstinate, and your nerves are strong, till not one of your soldiers or your sailors is left. On my word of honour, as a gentleman-buccanier, I promise you that. Ask my men if I ever broke my word.'

He rested the barrel of the pistol against Tom Packer's head, and looked at his watch, as perfectly composed, in his cat-like cruelty, as if he was waiting for the boiling of an egg.

'If you think it best not to answer him, ladies,' says Tom, 'never mind me. It's my trade to risk my life; and I shall lose it in a good cause.'

'A brave man,' said the Pirate Captain, lightly. 'Well, ladies, are you going to sacrifice the brave man?'

'We are going to save him,' said Miss Maryon, 'as he has striven to save us. *I* belong to the captain of the sloop. I am his sister.' She stopped, and whispered anxiously to Mrs Macey, who was standing with her. 'Don't acknowledge yourself, as I have done – you have children.'

'Good!' said the Pirate Captain. 'The answer is given, and the brains may stop in the brave man's head.' He put his watch and pistol back, and took two or three quick puffs at his cigar to keep it alight – then handed the paper he had written on, and his penfull of ink, to Miss Maryon.

'Read that over,' he said, 'and sign it for yourself, and the women and children with you.'

Saying those words, he turned round briskly on his heel, and began talking, in a whisper, to Giant-Georgy, the big English mate. What he was talking about, of course, I could not hear; but I noticed that he motioned several times straight into the interior of the country.

'Davis,' said Miss Maryon, 'look at this.'

She crossed before her sister, as she spoke, and held the paper which the Pirate Captain had given to her, under my eyes – my bound arms not allowing me to take it myself. Never to my dying day shall I forget the shame I felt, when I was obliged to acknowledge to Miss Maryon that I could not read a word of it!

'There are better men than me, ma'am,' I said, with a sinking heart, 'who can read it, and advise you for the best.'

'None better,' she answered, quietly. 'None, whose advice I would so willingly take. I have seen enough, to feel sure of that. Listen, Davis, while I read.'

Her pale face turned paler still, as she fixed her eyes on the paper. Lowering her voice to a whisper, so that the women and children near might not hear, she read me these lines:

To the Captains of English men-of-war, and to the commanders of vessels of other nations, cruising in the Caribbean Seas.

The precious metal and the jewels laid up in the English Island of Silver-Store, are in the possession of the Buccaniers, at sea.

The women and children of the Island of Silver-Store, to the number of Twenty-Two, are in the possession of the Buccaniers, on land.

They will be taken up the country, with fourteen men prisoners (whose lives the Buccaniers have private reasons of their own for preserving), to a place of confinement, which is unapproachable by strangers. They will be kept there until a certain day, previously agreed on between the Buccaniers at sea, and the Buccaniers on land.

If, by that time, no news from the party at sea, reaches the party on land, it will be taken for granted that the expedition which conveys away the silver and jewels has been met, engaged, and conquered by superior force; that the Treasure has been taken from its present owners; and that the Buccaniers guarding it, have been made prisoners, to be dealt with according to the law.

The absence of the expected news at the appointed time, being interpreted in this way, it will be the next object of the Buccaniers on land to take reprisals for the loss and the injury inflicted on their companions at sea. The lives of the women and children of the Island of Silver-Store are absolutely at their mercy; and those lives will pay the forfeit, if the Treasure is taken away, and if the men in possession of it come to harm.

This paper will be nailed to the lid of the largest chest taken from the Island. Any officer whom the chances of war may bring within reading distance of it, is warned to pause and consider, before his conduct signs the death warrant of the women and children of an English colony.

Signed, under the Black Flag,
PEDRO MENDEZ,

Commander of the Buccaniers, and Chief of the Guard over the English Prisoners.

The statement above written, in so far as it regards the situation we are now placed in, may be depended on as the truth.

Signed, on behalf of the imprisoned women and children of the Island of Silver-Store.

'Beneath this last line,' said Miss Maryon, pointing to it, 'is a blank space, in which I am expected to sign my name.'

'And in five minutes' time,' added the Pirate Captain, who had stolen close up to us, 'or the same consequences will follow which I had the pleasure of explaining to you a few minutes ago.'

He again drew out his watch and pistol; but, this time, it was my head that he touched with the barrel.

'When Tom Packer spoke for himself, miss, a little while ago,' I said, 'please to consider that he spoke for me.'

'Another brave man!' said the Pirate Captain, with his ape's grin. 'Am I to fire my pistol this time, or am I to put it back again as I did before?'

Miss Maryon did not seem to hear him. Her kind eyes rested for a moment on my face, and then looked up to the bright Heaven above us.

'Whether I sign, or whether I do not sign,' she said, 'we are still in the hands of God, and the future which His wisdom has appointed will not the less surely come.'

With those words she placed the paper on my breast, signed it, and handed it back to the Pirate Captain.

'This is our secret, Davis,' she whispered. 'Let us keep the dreadful knowledge of it to ourselves as long as we can.'

I have another singular confession to make – I hardly expect anybody to believe me when I mention the circumstance – but it is not the less the plain truth that, even in the midst of that frightful situation, I felt, for a few moments, a sensation of happiness while Miss Maryon's hand was holding the paper on my breast, and while her lips were telling me that there was a secret between us which we were to keep together.

The Pirate Captain carried the signed paper at once to his mate.

47

'Go back to the Island,' he says, 'and nail that with your own hands on the lid of the largest chest. There is no occasion to hurry the business of shipping the Treasure, because there is nobody on the Island to make signals that may draw attention to it from the sea. I have provided for that; and I have provided for the chance of your being outmanœuvred afterwards, by English, or other cruisers. Here are your sailing orders' (he took them from his pocket while he spoke), 'your directions for the disposal of the Treasure, and your appointment of the day and the place for communicating again with me and my prisoners. I have done my part – go you, now, and do yours.'

Hearing the clearness with which he gave his orders; knowing what the devilish scheme was that he had invented for preventing the recovery of the Treasure, even if our ships happened to meet and capture the pirates at sea; remembering what the look and the speech of him had been, when he put his pistol to my head and Tom Packer's; I began to understand how it was that this little, weak, weazen, wicked spider had got the first place and kept it among the villains about him.

The mate moved off, with his orders, towards the sea. Before he got there, the Pirate Captain beckoned another of the crew to come to him; and spoke a few words in his own, or in some other foreign language. I guessed what they meant, when I saw thirty of the pirates told off together, and set in a circle all round us. The rest were marched away after the mate. In the same manner the Sambos were divided next. Ten, including Christian George King, were left with us; and the others were sent down to the canoes. When this had been done, the Pirate Captain looked at his watch; pointed to some trees, about a mile off, which fringed the land as it rose from the beach; said to an American among the pirates round us, who seemed to hold the place of second mate, 'In two hours from this time;' and then walked away briskly, with one of his men after him, to some baggage piled up below us on the beach.

We were marched off at once to the shady place under the trees, and allowed to sit down there, in the cool, with our guard in a ring round us. Feeling certain from what I saw, and from what I knew to be contained in the written paper signed by Miss Maryon, that we were on the point of undertaking a long journey up the country, I anxiously examined my fellow prisoners to see how fit they looked for encountering bodily hardship and fatigue: to say nothing of mental suspense and terror, over and above.

With all possible respect for an official gentleman, I must admit that Mr Commissioner Pordage struck me as being, beyond any comparison, the most helpless individual in our unfortunate company. What with the fright he had suffered, the danger he had gone through, and the bewilderment of finding himself torn clean away from his safe Government moorings, his poor unfortunate brains seemed to be as completely discomposed as his Diplomatic coat. He was perfectly harmless and quiet, but also perfectly light-headed – as anybody could discover who looked at his dazed eyes or listened to his maundering talk. I tried him with a word or two about our miserable situation; thinking that, if any subject would get a trifle of sense out of him, it must surely be that.

'You will observe,' said Mr Pordage, looking at the torn cuffs of his Diplomatic coat instead of at me, 'that I cannot take cognisance of our situation. No memorandum of it has been drawn up; no report in connexion with it has been presented to me. I cannot possibly recognise it until the necessary minutes and memorandums and reports have reached me through the proper channels. When our miserable situation presents itself to me, on paper, I shall bring it under the notice of Government; and Government, after a proper interval, will bring it back again under my notice; and then I shall have something to say about it. Not a minute before, – no, my man, not a minute before!'

Speaking of Mr Pordage's wanderings of mind, reminds me that it is necessary to say a word next, about the much more serious case of Serjeant Drooce. The cut on his head, acted on by the heat of the climate, had driven him, to all appearance, stark mad. Besides the danger to himself, if he broke out before the Pirates, there was the danger to the women and children, of trusting him among them – a misfortune which, in our captive condition, it was impossible to avoid. Most providentially, however (as I found on inquiry) Tom Packer, who had saved his life, had a power of controlling him, which none of the rest of us possessed. Some shattered recollection of the manner in which he had been preserved from death, seemed to be still left in a corner of his memory. Whenever he showed symptoms of breaking out, Tom looked at him, and repeated with his hand and arm the action of cutting out right and left which had been the means of his saving the serjeant. On seeing that, Drooce always huddled himself up close to Tom, and fell silent. We, – that is, Packer and I – arranged it together that he was always to keep near Drooce, whatever happened, and however far we might be marched before we reached the place of our imprisonment.

The rest of us men – meaning Mr Macey, Mr Fisher, two of my comrades of the Marines, and five of the sloop's crew – were, making allowance for a little smarting in our wounds, in tolerable health, and not half so much broken in spirit by troubles, past, present, and to come, as some persons might be apt to imagine. As for the seamen, especially, no stranger who looked at their jolly brown faces would ever have imagined that they were prisoners, and in peril of their lives. They sat together, chewing their quids,[38] and looking out good-humouredly at the sea, like a gang of liberty-men resting themselves on shore. 'Take it easy, soldier,' says one of the six, seeing me looking at him. 'And, if you can't do that, take it as easy as you can.' I thought, at the time, that many a wiser man might have given me less sensible advice than this, though it was only offered by a boatswain's mate.

A movement among the Pirates attracted my notice to the beach below us, and I saw their Captain approaching our halting place, having changed his fine clothes for garments that were fit to travel in.

His coming back to us had the effect of producing unmistakable signs of preparation for a long journey. Shortly after he appeared, three Indians came up, leading three loaded mules; and these were followed, in a few minutes, by two of the Sambos, carrying between them a copper full of smoking meat and broth. After having been shared among the Pirates, this mess was set down before us, with some wooden bowls floating about in it, to dip out the food with. Seeing that we hesitated before touching it, the Pirate Captain recommended us not to be too mealy-mouthed, as that was meat from our own stores on the Island, and the last we were likely to taste for a long time to come. The sailors, without any more ado about it, professed their readiness to follow this advice, muttering among themselves that good meat was a good thing, though the devil himself had cooked it. The Pirate Captain then, observing that we were all ready to accept the food, ordered the bonds that confined the hands of us men to be loosened and cast off, so that we might help ourselves. After we had served the women and children, we fell to. It was a good meal

– though I can't say that I myself had much appetite for it. Jack, to use his own phrase, stowed away a double allowance. The jolly faces of the seamen lengthened a good deal, however, when they found there was nothing to drink afterwards but plain water. One of them, a fat man, named Short, went so far as to say that, in the turn things seemed to have taken, he should like to make his will before we started, as the stoppage of his grog[39] and the stoppage of his life were two events that would occur uncommonly close together.

When we had done, we were all ordered to stand up. The Pirates approached me and the other men, to bind our arms again; but, the Captain stopped them.

'No,' says he. 'I want them to get on at a good pace; and they will do that best with their arms free. Now, prisoners,' he continued, addressing us, 'I don't mean to have any lagging on the road. I have fed you up with good meat, and you have no excuse for not stepping out briskly – women, children, and all. You men are without weapons and without food, and you know nothing of the country you are going to travel through. If you are mad enough, in this helpless condition, to attempt escaping on the march, you will be shot, as sure as you all stand there, – and if the bullet misses, you will starve to death in forests that have no path and no end.'

Having addressed us in those words, he turned again to his men. I wondered then, as I had wondered once or twice already, what those private reasons might be, which he had mentioned in his written paper, for sparing the lives of us male prisoners. I hoped he would refer to them now – but I was disappointed.

'While the country allows it,' he went on, addressing his crew, 'march in a square, and keep the prisoners inside. Whether it is man, woman, or child, shoot any one of them who tries to escape, on peril of being shot yourselves if you miss. Put the Indians and mules in front, and the Sambos next to them. Draw up the prisoners all together. Tell off seven men to march before them, and seven more for each side; and leave the other nine for the rearguard. A fourth mule for me, when I get tired, and another Indian to carry my guitar.'

His guitar! To think of the murderous thief having a turn for strumming tunes, and wanting to cultivate it on such an expedition as ours! I could hardly believe my eyes when I saw the guitar brought forward in a neat green case, with the piratical skull and crossbones[40] and the Pirate Captain's initials painted on it in white.

'I can stand a good deal,' whispers Tom Packer to me, looking hard at the guitar; 'but confound me, Davis, if it's not a trifle too much to be taken prisoner by such a fellow as that!'

The Pirate Captain lights another cigar.

'March!' says he, with a screech like a cat, and a flourish with his sword, of the sort that a stage player would give at the head of a mock army.

We all moved off, leaving the clump of trees to the right, going, we knew not whither, to unknown sufferings and an unknown fate. The land that lay before us was wild and open, without fences or habitations. Here and there, cattle wandered about over it, and a few stray Indians. Beyond, in the distance, as far as we could see, rose a prospect of mountains and forests. Above us, was the pitiless sun, in a sky that was too brightly blue to look at. Behind us, was the calm murmuring ocean, with the dear island home which the women and children had lost, rising in the distance like a little green garden on the bosom of the sea. After half an hour's walking, we began to descend into the plain, and the last glimpse of the Island of Silver-Store disappeared from our view.

The order of march which we prisoners now maintained among ourselves, being the order which, with certain occasional variations, we observed for the next three days, I may as well give some description of it in this place, before I get occupied with other things, and forget it.

I myself, and the sailor I have mentioned under the name of Short, led the march. After us came Miss Maryon, and Mr and Mrs Macey. They were followed by two of my comrades of the Marines, with Mrs Pordage, Mrs Belltott, and two of the strongest of the ladies to look after them. Mr Fisher, the ship's boy, and the three remaining men of the sloop's crew, with the rest of the women and children came next; Tom Packer, taking care of Serjeant Drooce, brought up the rear. So long as we got on quickly enough, the pirates showed no disposition to interfere with our order of march; but, if there were any signs of lagging – and God knows it was hard enough work for a man to walk under that burning sun! – the villains threatened the weakest of our company with the points of their swords. The younger among the children gave out, as might have been expected, poor things, very early on the march. Short and I set the example of taking two of them up, pick-a-back, which was followed directly by the rest of the men. Two of Mrs Macey's three children fell to our share; the eldest, travelling behind us on his father's back. Short hoisted the next in age, a girl, on his broad shoulders. I see him now as if it was yesterday, with the perspiration pouring down his fat face and bushy whiskers, rolling along as if he was on the deck of a ship, and making a sling of his neck-handkerchief, with his clever sailor's fingers, to support the little girl on his back. 'I expect you'll marry me, my darling, when you grow up,' says he, in his oily, joking voice. And the poor child, in her innocence, laid her weary head down on his shoulder, and gravely and faithfully promised that she would.

A lighter weight fell to my share. I had the youngest of the children, the pretty little boy, already mentioned, who had been deaf and dumb from his birth. His mother's voice trembled sadly, as she thanked me for taking him up, and tenderly put his little dress right while she walked behind me. 'He is very little and light of his age,' says the poor lady, trying hard to speak steady. 'He won't give you much trouble, Davis – he has always been a very patient child from the first.' The boy's little frail arms clasped themselves round my neck while she was speaking; and something or other seemed to stop in my throat the cheerful answer that I wanted to make. I walked on with what must have looked, I am afraid, like a gruff silence; the poor child humming softly on my back, in his unchanging, dumb way, till he hummed himself to sleep. Often and often, since that time, in dreams, I have felt those small arms round my neck again, and have heard that dumb murmuring song in my ear, dying away fainter and fainter, till nothing was left but the light breath rising and falling regularly on my cheek, telling me that my little fellow prisoner had forgotten his troubles in sleep.

We marched, as well as I could guess, somewhere about seven miles that day – a short spell enough, judging by distance, but a terrible long one judging by heat. Our halting place was by the banks of a stream, across which, at a little distance, some wild pigs were swimming as we came up. Beyond us, was the same view of forests and mountains that I have already mentioned; and all round us, was a perfect wilderness of flowers. The shrubs, the bushes, the ground, all blazed again with magnificent colours, under the evening sun. When we were ordered to halt, wherever we set a child down, there that child had laps and laps full of flowers growing within reach of its hand. We sat on flowers, eat on flowers, slept at night on flowers – any chance handful of which would have been well worth a golden guinea among the gentlefolks in England. It was a sight not easily described, to see niggers, savages, and Pirates, hideous, filthy, and ferocious in the last degree to look at, squatting about grimly upon a natural carpet of beauty, of the sort that is painted in pictures with pretty fairies dancing on it.

The mules were unloaded, and left to roll among the flowers to their hearts' content. A neat tent was set up for the Pirate Captain, at the door of which, after eating a good meal, he laid himself down in a languishing attitude, with a nosegay in the bosom of his waistcoat, and his guitar on his knees, and jingled away at the strings, singing foreign songs, with a shrill voice and with his nose conceitedly turned up in the air. I was obliged to caution Short and the sailors – or they would, to a dead certainty, have put all our lives in peril by openly laughing at him.

We had but a poor supper that night. The Pirates now kept the provisions they had brought from the Island, for their own use; and we had to share the miserable starvation diet of the country, with the Indians and the Sambos. This consisted of black beans fried, and of things they call Tortillas, meaning, in plain English, flat cakes made of crushed Indian corn, and baked on a clay griddle. Not only was this food insipid, but the dirty manner in which the Indians prepared it, was disgusting. However, complaint was useless; for we could see for ourselves that no other provision had been brought for the prisoners. I heard some grumbling among our men, and some little fretfulness among the children, which their mothers soon quieted. I myself was indifferent enough to the quality of the food; for I had noticed a circumstance, just before it was brought to us, which occupied my mind with more serious considerations. One of the mules was unloaded near us, and I observed among the baggage a large bundle of new axes, doubtless taken from some ship. After puzzling my brains for some time to know what they could be wanted for, I came to the conclusion that they were to be employed in cutting our way through, when we came to the forests. To think of the kind of travelling which these preparations promised – if the view I took of them was the right one – and then to look at the women and children, exhausted by the first day's march, was sufficient to make any man uneasy. It weighed heavily enough on my mind, I know, when I woke up among the flowers, from time to time, that night.

Our sleeping arrangements, though we had not a single civilised comfort, were, thanks to the flowers, simple and easy enough. For the first time in their lives, the women and children laid down together, with the sky for a roof, and the kind earth for a bed. We men shook ourselves down, as well as we could, all round them; and the Pirates, relieving guard regularly, ranged themselves outside of all. In that tropical climate, and at that hot time, the night was only pleasantly cool. The bubbling of the stream, and, now and then, the course of the breeze through the flowers, was all we heard. During the hours of darkness, it occurred to me – and I have no doubt the same idea struck my comrades – that a body of determined men, making a dash for it, might now have stood a fair chance of escaping. We were still near enough to the seashore to be certain of not losing our way; and the plain was almost as smooth, for a good long run, as a natural racecourse. However, the mere act of dwelling on such a notion, was waste of time and thought, situated as we were with regard to the women and children. They were, so to speak, the hostages who insured our submission to captivity, or to any other hardship that might be inflicted on us; a result which I have no doubt the Pirate Captain had foreseen, when he made us all prisoners together on taking possession of the Island.

We were roused up at four in the morning, to travel on before the heat set in; our march under yesterday's broiling sun having been only undertaken for the purpose of getting us away from the seashore, and from possible help in that quarter, without loss of time. We forded the stream, wading through it waist-deep: except the children, who crossed on our shoulders. An hour before noon, we halted under two immense wild cotton trees, about half a mile from a little brook, which probably ran into the stream we had passed in the morning. Late in the afternoon we were on foot again, and encamped for the night at three deserted huts, built of mud and poles. There were the remains of an enclosure here, intended, as I thought, for cattle; and there was an old well, from which our supply of water was got. The greater part of the women were very tired and sorrowful that night; but Miss Maryon did wonders in cheering them up.

On the third morning, we began to skirt the edge of a mountain, carrying our store of water with us from the well. We men prisoners had our full share of the burden. What with that, what with the way being all uphill, and what with the necessity of helping on the weaker members of our company, that day's march was the hardest I remember to have ever got through. Towards evening, after resting again in the middle of the day, we stopped for the night on the verge of the forest. A dim, lowering, awful sight it was, to look up at the mighty wall of trees, stretching in front, and on either side of us without a limit and without a break. Through the night, though there was no wind blowing over our encampment, we heard deep, moaning, rushing sounds rolling about, at intervals, in the great inner wilderness of leaves; and, now and then, those among us who slept, were startled up by distant crashes in the depths of the forest – the death knells of falling trees. We kept fires alight, in case of wild animals stealing out on us in the darkness; and the flaring red light, and the thick, winding smoke, alternately showed and hid the forest prospect in a strangely treacherous and ghostly way. The children shuddered with fear; even the Pirate Captain forgot, for the first time, to jingle his eternal guitar.

When we were mustered in the morning for the march, I fully expected to see the axes unpacked. To my surprise they were not disturbed. The Indians drew their long chopping knives (called machetes in the language of that country); made for a place among the trees where I could see no signs of a path; and began cutting at the bushes and shrubs, and at the wild vines and creepers, twirling down together in all sorts of fantastic forms, from the lofty branches. After clearing a few dozen yards inwards they came out to us again, whooping and showing their wicked teeth, as they laid hold of the mules' halters to lead them on. The Pirate Captain, before we moved after, took out a pocket compass, set it, pondered over it for some time, shrugged his shoulders, and screeched out 'March', as usual. We entered the forest, leaving behind us the last chance of escape, and the last hope of ever getting back to the regions of humanity and civilisation. By this time, we had walked inland, as nearly as I could estimate, about thirty miles.

The order of our march was now, of necessity, somewhat changed. We all followed each other in a long line, shut in, however, as before, in front and in rear, by the Indians, the Sambos, and the pirates. Though none of us could see a vestige of any path, it was clear that our guides knew where they were going; for, we were never stopped by any obstacles, except the shrubs and wild vines which they could cut through with their chopping knives. Sometimes, we marched under great branches which met like arches high over our heads. Sometimes, the boughs were so low that we had to stoop to pass under them. Sometimes, we wound in and out among mighty trunks of trees, with their gnarled roots twisting up far above the ground, and with creepers in full flower twining down in hundreds from their lofty branches. The size of the leaves and the countless multitude of the trees shut out the sun, and made a solemn dimness which it was awful and without hope to walk through. Hours would pass without our hearing a sound but the dreary rustle of our own feet over the leafy ground. At other times, whole troops of parrots,[41] with feathers of all the colours of the rainbow, chattered and shrieked at us; and processions of monkeys[42], fifty or sixty at a time, followed our progress in the boughs overhead: passing through the thick leaves with a sound like the rush of a steady wind. Every now and then, the children were startled by lizard-like creatures, three feet long, running up the trunks of the trees as we passed by them; more than once, swarms of locusts tormented us, startled out of their hiding places by the monkeys in the boughs. For five days we marched incessantly through this dismal forest region, only catching a clear glimpse of the sky above us, on three occasions in all that time. The distance we walked each day seemed to be regulated by the positions of springs and streams in the forest, which the Indians knew of. Sometimes those springs and streams lay near together; and our day's work was short. Sometimes they were far apart; and the march was long and weary. On all occasions, two of the Indians, followed by two of the Sambos, disappeared as soon as we encamped for the night; and returned, in a longer or shorter time, bringing water with them. Towards the latter part of the journey, weariness had so completely mastered the weakest among our company, that they ceased to take notice of anything. They walked without looking to the right or to the left, and they eat their wretched food and lay down to sleep with a silent despair that was shocking. Mr Pordage left off maundering now, and Serjeant Drooce was so quiet and biddable, that Tom Packer had an easy time of it with him at last. Those among us who still talked, began to get a habit of dropping our voices to a whisper. Short's jokes languished and dwindled; Miss Maryon's voice, still kind and tender as ever, began to lose its clearness; and the poor children, when they got weary and cried, shed tears silently, like old people. It seemed as if the darkness and the hush of the endless forest had cast its shadow on our spirits, and had stolen drearily into our inmost hearts.

On the sixth day, we saw the blessed sunshine on the ground before us, once more. Prisoners as we were, there was a feeling of freedom on stepping into the light again, and on looking up, without interruption, into the clear blue Heaven, from which no human creature can keep any other human creature, when the time comes for rising to it. A turn in the path brought us out suddenly at an Indian village – a wretched place, made up of two rows of huts built with poles, the crevices between them stopped with mud, and the roofs thatched in the coarsest manner with palm leaves. The savages squatted about, jumped to their feet in terror as we came in view; but, seeing the Indians at the head of our party, took heart, and began chattering and screeching, just like the parrots we had left in the forest. Our guides answered in their gibberish; some lean, half-wild dogs yelped and howled incessantly; and the Pirates discharged their muskets and loaded them again, to make sure that their powder had not got damp on the march. No want of muskets among them now! The noise and the light and the confusion, after the silence, darkness, and discipline that we had been used to for the last five days, so bewildered us all, that it was quite a relief to sit down on the ground and let the guard about us shut out our view on every side.

'Davis! Are we at the end of the march?' says Miss Maryon, touching my arm.

The other women looked anxiously at me, as she put the question. I got on my feet, and saw the Pirate Captain communicating with the Indians of the village. His hands were making signs in the fussy foreign way, all the time he was speaking. Sometimes, they pointed away to where the forest began again beyond us; and sometimes they went up both together to his mouth, as if he was wishful of getting a fresh supply of the necessaries of life.

My eyes next turned towards the mules. Nobody was employed in unpacking the baggage; nobody went near that bundle of axes which had weighed on my mind so much already, and the mystery of which still tormented me in secret. I came to the conclusion that we were not yet at the end of our journey; I communicated my opinion to Miss Maryon. She got up herself, with my help, and looked about her, and made the remark, very justly, that all the huts in the village would not suffice to hold us. At the same time, I pointed out to her that the mule which the Pirate Captain had ridden had been relieved of his saddle, and was being led away, at that moment, to a patch of grass behind one of the huts.

'That looks as if we were not going much farther on,' says I.

'Thank Heaven if it be so, for the sake of the poor children!' says Miss Maryon. 'Davis, suppose something happened which gave us a chance of escaping? Do you think we could ever find our way back to the sea?'

'Not a hope of getting back, miss. If the Pirates were to let us go this very instant, those pathless forests would keep us in prison forever.'

'Too true! Too true!' she said, and said no more.

In another half-hour we were roused up, and marched away from the village (as I had thought we should be) into the forest again. This time, though there was by no means so much cutting through the underwood needed as in our previous experience, we were accompanied by at least a dozen Indians, who seemed to me to be following us out of sheer idleness and curiosity. We had walked, as well as I could calculate, more than an hour, and I was trudging along with the little deaf-and-dumb boy on my back, as usual, thinking, not very hopefully, of our future prospects, when I was startled by a moan in my ear from the child. One of his arms was trembling round my neck, and the other pointed away towards my right hand. I looked in that direction – and there, as if it had started up out of the ground to dispute our passage through the forest, was a hideous monster carved in stone, twice my height at least. The thing loomed out of a ghostly white, against the dark curtain of trees all round it. Spots of rank moss stuck about over its great glaring stone face; its stumpy hands were tucked up into its breast; its legs and feet were four times the size of any human limbs; its body and the flat space of spare stone which rose above its head, were all covered with mysterious devices – little grinning men's faces, heads of crocodiles and apes, twisting knots and twirling knobs, strangely shaped leaves, winding latticework; legs, arms, fingers, toes, skulls, bones, and such like. The monstrous statue leaned over on one side, and was only kept from falling to the ground by the roots of a great tree which had wound themselves all round the lower half of it. Altogether, it was as horrible and ghastly an object to come upon suddenly, in the unknown depths of a great forest, as the mind (or, at all events, my mind) can conceive. When I say that the first meeting with the statue struck me speechless, nobody can wonder that the children actually screamed with terror at the sight of it.

'It's only a great big doll, my darling,' says Short, at his wit's end how to quiet the little girl on his back. 'We'll get a nice soft bit of wood soon, and show these nasty savages how to make a better one.'

While he was speaking, Miss Maryon was close behind me, soothing the deaf-and-dumb boy by signs which I could not understand.

'I have heard of these things, Davis,' she says. 'They are idols, made by a lost race of people, who lived, no one can say how many hundred or how many thousand years ago. That hideous thing was carved and worshipped while the great tree that now supports it was yet a seed in the ground. We must get the children used to these stone monsters. I believe we are coming to many more of them. I believe we are close to the remains of one of those mysterious ruined cities which have long been supposed to exist in this part of the world.' [43]

Before I could answer, the word of command from the rear drove us on again. In passing the idol, some of the Pirates fired their muskets at it. The echoes from the reports rang back on us with a sharp rattling sound. We pushed on a few paces, when the Indians ahead suddenly stopped, flourished their chopping knives, and all screamed out together 'El Palacio!' The Englishmen among the Pirates took up the cry, and, running forward through the trees on either side of us, roared out, 'The Palace!' Other voices joined theirs in other tongues; and, for a minute or two, there was a general confusion of everybody, – the first that had occurred since we were marched away, prisoners, from the seashore.

I tightened my hold of the child on my back; took Miss Maryon closer to me, to save her from being roughly jostled by the men about us; and marched up as near to the front as the press and the trees would let me. Looking over the heads of the Indians, and between the trunks, I beheld a sight which I shall never forget: no, not to my dying day.

A wilderness of ruins spread out before me, overrun by a forest of trees. In every direction, look where I would, a frightful confusion of idols, pillars, blocks of stone, heavy walls, and flights of steps, met my eye; some, whole and upright; others, broken and scattered on the ground; and all, whatever their condition, overgrown and clasped about by roots, branches, and curling vines, that writhed round them like so many great snakes. Every here and there, strange buildings stood up, with walls on the tops of which three men might have marched abreast – buildings with their roofs burst off or tumbled in, and with the trees springing up from inside, and waving their restless shadows mournfully over the ruins. High in the midst of this desolation, towered a broad platform of rocky earth, scarped[44] away on three sides, so as to make it unapproachable except by scaling ladders. On the fourth side, the flat of the platform was reached by a flight of stone steps, of such mighty size and strength that they might have been made for the use of a race of giants. They led to a huge building girded all round with a row of thick pillars, long enough and broad enough to cover the whole flat space of ground; solid enough, as to the walls, to stand forever; but broken in, at most places, as to the roof; and overshadowed by the trees that sprang up from inside, like the smaller houses already mentioned, below it. This was the dismal ruin which was called the Palace; and this was the Prison in the Woods which was to be the place of our captivity.

The screeching voice of the Pirate Captain restored order in our ranks, and sent the Indians forward with their chopping knives to the steps of the Palace. We were directed to follow them across the ruins, and in and out among the trees. Out of every ugly crevice and crack in the great stairs, there sprouted up flowers, long grasses, and beautiful large-leaved plants and bushes. When we had toiled to the top of the flight, we could look back from the height over the dark waving top of the forest behind us. More than a glimpse of the magnificent sight, however, was not allowed: we were ordered still to follow the Indians. They had already disappeared in the inside of the Palace; and we went in after them.

We found ourselves, first, under a square portico, supported upon immense flat slabs of stone, which were carved all over, at top and bottom, with death's-heads set in the midst of circles of sculptured flowers. I guessed the length of the portico to be, at the very least, three hundred feet. In the inside wall of it, appeared four high gaping doorways; three of them were entirely choked up by fallen stones: so jammed together, and so girt about by roots and climbing plants, that no force short of a blast of gunpowder, could possibly have dislodged them. The fourth entrance had, at some former time, been kept just clear enough to allow of the passing of one man at once through the gap that had been made in the fallen stones. Through this, the only passage left into the Palace, or out of it, we followed the Indians into a great hall, nearly one half of which was still covered by the remains of the roof. In the unsheltered half: surrounded by broken stones and with a carved human head, five times the size of life, leaning against it: rose the straight, naked trunk of a beautiful tree, that shot up high above the ruins, and dropped its enormous branches from the very top of it, bending down towards us, in curves like plumes of immense green feathers. In this hall, which was big enough to hold double our number, we were ordered to make a halt, while the Pirate Captain, accompanied by three of his crew, followed the Indians through a doorway, leading off to the left hand, as we stood with our backs to the portico. In front of us, towards the right, was another doorway, through which we could see some of the Indians, cutting away with their knives, right and left, at the overspreading underwood. Even the noise of the hacking, and the hum and murmur of the people outside, who were unloading the mules, seemed to be sounds too faint and trifling to break the awful stillness of the ruins. To my ears, at least, the unearthly silence was deepened rather than broken by the few feeble sounds which tried to disturb it. The wailings of the poor children were stifled within them. The whispers of the women, and the heavy breathing of the overlaboured men, sank and sank gradually till they were heard no more. Looking back now, at the whole course of our troubles, I think I can safely say that nothing – not even the first discovery of the treachery on the Island – tried our courage and endurance like that interval of speechless waiting in the Palace, with the hush of the ruined city, and the dimness of the endless forest, all about us.

When we next saw the Pirate Captain, he appeared at the doorway to the right, just as the Pirates began to crowd in from the portico, with the baggage they had taken from the mules.

'There is the way for the Buccaniers,' squeaks the Pirate Captain, addressing the American mate, and pointing to the doorway on the left. 'Three big rooms, that will hold you all, and that have more of the roof left on them than any of the others. The prisoners,' he continues, turning to us, and pointing to the doorway behind him, 'will file in, that way, and will find two rooms for them, with the ceilings on the floor, and the trees in their places. I myself, because my soul is big, shall live alone in this grand hall. My bed shall be there in the sheltered corner; and I shall eat, and drink, and smoke, and sing, and enjoy myself, with one eye always on my prisoners, and the other eye always on my guard outside.'

Having delivered this piece of eloquence, he pointed with his sword to the prisoners' doorway. We all passed through it quickly, glad to be out of the sight and hearing of him.

The two rooms set apart for us, communicated with each other. The inner one of the two had a second doorway, lead-ing, as I supposed, further into the building, but so choked up by rubbish, as to be impassable, except by climbing, and that must have been skilful climbing too. Seeing that this accident cut off all easy means of approach to the room from the Pirates' side, we determined, supposing nobody meddled with us, to establish the women and children here; and to take the room nearest to the Pirate Captain and his guard for ourselves.

The first thing to be done was to clear away the rubbish in the women's room. The ceiling was, indeed, as the Pirate Captain had told us, all on the floor; and the growth of trees, shrubs, weeds, and flowers, springing up everywhere among the fragments of stone, was so prodigious in this part of the Palace, that, but for the walls with their barbarous sculptures all round, we should certainly have believed ourselves to be encamped in the forest, without a building near us. All the lighter parts of the rubbish in the women's room we disposed of, cleverly, by piling it in the doorway on the Pirates' side, so as to make any approach from that direction all but impossible, even by climbing. The heavy blocks of stone– and it took two men to lift some of them that were not the heaviest – we piled up in the middle of the floor. Having by this means cleared away plenty of space round the walls, we gathered up all the litter of young branches, bushes, and leaves which the Indians had chopped away; added to them as much as was required of the underwood still standing; and laid the whole smooth and even, to make beds. I noticed, while we were at this work, that the ship's boy – whose name was Robert – was particularly helpful and considerate with the children, when it became necessary to quiet them and to get them to lie down. He was a rough boy to look at, and not very sharp; but, he managed better, and was more naturally tender-hearted with the little ones than any of the rest of us. This may seem a small thing to mention; but Robert's attentive ways with the children, attached them to him; and that attachment, as will be hereafter shown, turned out to be of great benefit to us, at a very dangerous and very important time.

Our next piece of work was to clear our own room. It was close at the side of the Palace; and a break in the outward wall looked down over the sheer precipice on which the building stood. We stopped this up, breast high, in case of accidents, with the rubbish on the floor; we then made our beds, just as we had made the women's beds already.

A little later, we heard the Pirate Captain in the hall, which he kept to himself for his big soul and his little body, giving orders to the American mate about the guard. On mustering the Pirates, it turned out that two of them, who had been wounded in the fight on the Island, were unfit for duty. Twenty-eight, therefore, remained. These, the Pirate Captain divided into companies of seven, who were to mount guard, in turn, for a spell of six hours each company; the relief coming round, as a matter of course, four times in the twenty-four hours. Of the guard of seven, two were stationed under the portico; one was placed as a lookout, on the top landing of the great flight of steps; and two were appointed to patrol the ground below, in front of the Palace. This left only two men to watch the three remaining sides of the building. So far as any risks of attack were concerned, the precipices at the back and sides of the Palace were a sufficient defence for it, if a good watch was kept on the weak side. But what the Pirate Captain dreaded was the chance of our escaping; and he would not trust the precipices to keep us, knowing we had sailors in our company, and suspecting that they might hit on some substitute for ropes, and lower themselves and their fellow prisoners down from the back or the sides of the Palace, in the dark. Accordingly, the Pirate Captain settled it that two men out of each company should do double duty, after nightfall: the choice of them to be decided by casting dice. This gave four men to patrol round the sides and the back of the building: a sufficient number to keep a bright look-out. The Pirates murmured a little at the prospect of double duty; but, there was no remedy for it. The Indians, having a superstitious horror of remaining in the ruined city after dark, had bargained to be allowed to go back to their village, every afternoon. And, as for the Sambos, the Pirate Captain knew them better than the English had known them at Silver-Store, and would have nothing to do with them in any matter of importance.

The setting of the watch was completed without much delay. If any of us had felt the slightest hope of escaping, up to this time, the position of our prison and the number of sentinels appointed to guard it, would have been more than enough to extinguish that hope forever.

An hour before sunset, the Indians – whose only business at the Palace was to supply us with food from the village, and to prepare the food for eating – made their last batch of Tortillas, and then left the ruins in a body, at the usual trot of those savages when they are travelling in a hurry.

When the sun had set, the darkness came down upon us, I might almost say, with a rush. Bats whizzed about, and the low warning hum of Mosquitos sounded close to our ears. Flying beetles, with lights in their heads, each light as bright as the light of a dozen glowworms, sparkled through the darkness, in a wonderful manner, all night long. When one of them settled on the walls, he lighted up the hideous sculptures for a yard all round him, at the very least. Outside, in the forest, the dreadful stillness seemed to be drawing its breath, from time to time, when the night-wind swept lightly through the million-million leaves. Sometimes, the surge of monkeys travelling through the boughs, burst out with a sound like waves on a sandy shore; sometimes, the noise of falling branches and trunks rang out suddenly with a crash, as if the great ruins about us were splitting into pieces; sometimes, when the silence was at its deepest – when even the tread of the watch outside had ceased – the quick rustle of a lizard or a snake, sounded treacherously close at our ears. It was long before the children in the women's room were all quieted and hushed to sleep – longer still before we, their elders, could compose our spirits for the night. After all sounds died away among us, and when I thought that I was the only one still awake, I heard Miss Maryon's voice saying, softly, 'God help and deliver us!' A man in our room, moving on his bed of leaves, repeated the words after her; and the ship's boy, Robert, half-asleep, half-awake, whispered to himself sleepily, 'Amen!' After that, the silence returned upon us, and was broken no more. So the night passed – the first night in our Prison in the Woods.

71

With the morning, came the discovery of a new project of the Pirate Captain's, for which none of us had been prepared.

Soon after sunrise, the Pirate Captain looked into our room, and ordered all the men in it out into the large hall, where he lived with his big soul and his little body. After eyeing us narrowly, he directed three of the sailors, myself, and two of my comrades, to step apart from the rest. When we had obeyed, the bundle of axes which had troubled my mind so much, was brought into the hall; and four men of the guard, then on duty, armed with muskets and pistols, were marched in afterwards. Six of the axes were chosen and put into our hands, the Pirate Captain pointing warningly, as we took them, to the men with firearms in the front of us. He and his mate, both armed to the teeth, then led the way out to the steps; we followed; the other four Pirates came after us. We were formed, down the steps, in single file; the Pirate Captain at the head; I myself next to him; a Pirate next to me; and so on to the end, in such order as to keep a man with a loaded musket between each one or two of us prisoners. I looked behind me as we started, and saw two of the Sambos – that Christian George King was one of them – following us. We marched round the back of the Palace, and over the ruins beyond it, till we came to a track through the forest, the first I had seen. After a quarter of an hour's walking, I saw the sunlight, bright beyond the trees in front of us. In another minute or two, we stood under the clear sky, and beheld at our feet a broad river, running with a swift silent current, and overshadowed by the forest, rising as thick as ever on the bank that was opposite to us.

On the bank where we stood, the trees were young; some great tempest of past years having made havoc in this part of the forest, and torn away the old growth to make room for the new. The young trees grew up, mostly, straight and slender, –

72

that is to say, slender for South America, the slightest of them being, certainly, as thick as my leg. After peeping and peering about at the timber, with the look of a man who owned it all, the Pirate Captain sat himself down cross-legged on the grass, and did us the honour to address us.

'Aha! you English, what do you think I have kept you alive for?' says he. 'Because I am fond of you? Bah! Because I don't like to kill you? Bah! What for, then? Because I want the use of your arms to work for me. See those trees!' He waved his hand backwards and forwards, over the whole prospect. 'Cut them all down – lop off the branches – smooth them into poles – shape them into beams – chop them into planks. Camarado!' he went on, turning to the mate, 'I mean to roof in the Palace again, and to lay new floors over the rubbish of stones. I will make the big house good and dry to live in, in the rainy weather – I will barricade the steps of it for defence against an army, – I will make it my strong castle of retreat for me and my men, and our treasure, and our prisoners, and all that we have, when the English cruisers of the devil get too many for us along the coast. To work, you six! Look at those four men of mine, – their muskets are loaded. Look at these two Sambos who will stop here to fetch help if they want it. Remember the women and children you have left at the Palace – and at your peril and at their peril, turn those axes in your hands from their proper work! You understand? You English fools?'

With those words he jumped to his feet, and ordered the niggers to remain and place themselves at the orders of our guard. Having given these last directions, and having taken his mate's opinion as to whether three of the Buccaniers would not be enough to watch the Palace in the day, when the six stoutest men of the prisoners were away from it, the Pirate Captain offered his little weazen arm to the American, and strutted back to his castle, on better terms with himself than ever.

As soon as he and the mate were gone, Christian George King tumbled himself down on the grass, and kicked up his ugly heels in convulsions of delight.

'Oh, golly, golly, golly!' says he. 'You dam English do work, and Christian George King look on. Yup, Sojeer! whack at them tree!'

I paid no attention to the brute, being better occupied in noticing my next comrade, Short. I had remarked that all the while the Pirate Captain was speaking, he was looking hard at the river, as if the sight of a large sheet of water did his sailorly eyes good. When we began to use the axes, greatly to my astonishment, he buckled to at his work like a man who had his whole heart in it: chuckling to himself at every chop, and wagging his head as if he was in the forecastle[45] again telling his best yarns.

'You seem to be in spirits, Short?' I says, setting to on a tree close by him.

'The river's put a notion in my head,' says he. 'Chop away, Gill, as hard as you can, or they may hear us talking.'

'What notion has the river put in your head?' I asked that man, following his directions.

'You don't know where that river runs to, I suppose?' says Short. 'No more don't I. But, did it say anything particular to you, Gill, when you first set eyes on it? It said to *me,* as plain as words could speak, "I'm the road out of this. Come and try me!" – Steady! Don't stop to look at the water. Chop away, man, chop away.'

'The road out of this?' says I. 'A road without any coaches, Short. I don't see so much as the ruins of one old canoe lying about anywhere.'

Short chuckles again, and buries his axe in his tree.

'What are we cutting down these here trees for?' says he.

'Roofs and floors for the Pirate Captain's castle,' says I.

'Rafts for ourselves!' says he, with another tremendous chop at the tree, which brought it to the ground – the first that had fallen.

His words struck through me as if I had been shot. For the first time since our imprisonment I now saw, clear as daylight, a chance of escape. Only a chance, to be sure; but, still a chance.

Although the guard stood several paces away from us, and could by no possibility hear a word that we said, through the noise of the axes, Short was too cautious to talk any more.

'Wait till night,' he said, lopping the branches off the tree. 'Pass the word on in a whisper to the nearest of our men to work with a will; and say, with a wink of your eye, there's a good reason for it.'

After we had been allowed to knock off for that day, the Pirates had no cause to complain of the work we had done; and they reported us to the Pirate Captain as obedient and industrious, so far. When we lay down at night, I took the next place on the leaves to Short. We waited till the rest were asleep, and till we heard the Pirate Captain snoring in the great hall, before we began to talk again about the river and the rafts. This is the amount of what Short whispered in my ear on that occasion:

He told me he had calculated that it would take two large rafts to bear all our company, and that timber enough to make such two rafts might be cut down by six men in ten days, or, at most, in a fortnight. As for the means of fastening the rafts – the lashings, he called them – the stout vines and creepers supplied them abundantly; and the timbers of both rafts might be connected together, in this way, firmly enough for river navigation, in about five hours. That was the very shortest time the job would take, done by the willing hands of men who knew that they were working for their lives, said Short.

These were the means of escape. How to turn them to account was the next question. Short could not answer it; and though I tried all that night, neither could I.

The difficulty was one which, I think, might have puzzled wiser heads than ours. How were six-and-thirty living souls (being the number of us prisoners, including the children) to be got out of the Palace safely, in the face of the guard that watched it? And, even if that was accomplished, when could we count on gaining five hours all to ourselves for the business of making the rafts? The compassing of either of these two designs, absolutely necessary as they both were to our escape, seemed to be nothing more or less than a rank impossibility. Towards morning, I got a wild notion into my head about letting ourselves down from the back of the Palace, in the dark, and taking our chance of being able to seize the sentinels at that part of the building, unawares, and gag them before they could give the alarm to the Pirates in front. But, Short, when I mentioned my plan to him, would not hear of it. He said that men by themselves – provided they had not got a madman, like Drooce, and a maundering old gentleman, like Mr Pordage, among them – might, perhaps, run some such desperate risk as I proposed; but, that letting women and children, to say nothing of Drooce and Pordage, down a precipice in the dark, with makeshift ropes which might give way at a moment's notice, was out of the question. It was impossible, on further reflection, not to see that Short's view of the matter was the right one. I acknowledged as much, and then I put it to Short whether our wisest course would not be to let one or two of the sharpest of our fellow prisoners into our secret, and see what they said. Short asked me which two I had in my mind when I made that proposal?

'Mr Macey,' says I, 'because he is naturally quick, and has improved his gifts by learning, and Miss Maryon –'

'How can a woman help us?' says Short, breaking in on me.

'A woman with a clear head and a high courage and a patient resolution – all of which Miss Maryon has got, above all the world – may do more to help us, in our present strait, than any man of our company,' says I.

'Well,' says Short, 'I dare say you're right. Speak to anybody you please, Gill; but, whatever you do, man, stick to it at the trees. Let's get the timber down – that's the first thing to be done, anyhow.'

Before we were mustered for work, I took an opportunity of privately mentioning to Miss Maryon and Mr Macey what had passed between Short and me. They were both thunderstruck at the notion of the rafts. Miss Maryon, as I had expected, made lighter of the terrible difficulties in the way of carrying out our scheme than Mr Macey did.

'We are left here to watch and think, all day,' she whispered – and I could almost hear the quick beating of her heart. 'While you are making the best of your time among the trees, we will make the best of ours in the Palace. I can say no more, now – I can hardly speak at all for thinking of what you have told me. Bless you, bless you, for making me hope once more! Go now – we must not risk the consequences of being seen talking together. When you come back at night, look at me. If I close my eyes, it is a sign that nothing has been thought of yet. If I keep them open, take the first safe opportunity of speaking secretly to me or to Mr Macey.'

She turned away; and I went back to my comrades. Half an hour afterwards, we were off for our second day's work among the trees.

When we came back, I looked at Miss Maryon. She closed her eyes. So, nothing had been thought of, yet.

Six more days we worked at cutting down the trees, always meriting the same good character for industry from our Pirate guard. Six more evenings I looked at Miss Maryon; and six times her closed eyes gave me the same disheartening answer. On the ninth day of our work, Short whispered to me, that if we plied our axes for three days longer, he considered we should have more than timber enough down, to make the rafts. He had thought of nothing, I had thought of nothing, Miss Maryon and Mr Macey had thought of nothing. I was beginning to get low in spirits; but, Short was just as cool and easy as ever. 'Chop away, Davis,' was all he said. 'The river won't run dry yet awhile. Chop away!'

We knocked off, earlier than usual that day, the Pirates having a feast in prospect, off a wild hog. It was still broad daylight (out of the forest) when we came back, and when I looked once more in Miss Maryon's face.

I saw a flush in her cheeks; and her eyes met mine brightly. My heart beat quicker at the glance of them; for I saw that the time had come, and that the difficulty was conquered.

We waited till the light was fading, and the Pirates were in the midst of their feast. Then, she beckoned me into the inner room, and I sat down by her in the dimmest corner of it.

'You have thought of something, at last, Miss?'

'I have. But the merit of the thought is not all mine. Chance – no! Providence – suggested the design; and the instrument with which its merciful Wisdom has worked, is – a child.'

She stopped, and looked all round her anxiously, before she went on.

'This afternoon,' she says, 'I was sitting against the trunk of that tree, thinking of what has been the subject of my thoughts ever since you spoke to me. My sister's little girl was whiling away the tedious time, by asking Mr Kitten to tell her the names of the different plants which are still left growing about the room. You know he is a learned man in such matters?'

I knew that; and have, I believe, formerly given that out, for my Lady to take in writing.

'I was too much occupied,' she went on, 'to pay attention to them, till they came close to the tree against which I was sitting. Under it and about it, there grew a plant with very elegantly shaped leaves, and with a kind of berry on it. The child showed it to Mr Kitten; and saying, "Those berries look good to eat," stretched out her hand towards them. Mr Kitten stopped her. "You must never touch that," he said. "Why not?" the child asked. "Because if you eat much of it, it would poison you." "And if I only eat a little?" said the child, laughing. "If you only eat a little," said Mr Kitten, "it would throw you into a deep sleep – a sleep that none of us could wake you from, when it was time for breakfast – a sleep that would make your mama think you were dead." Those words were hardly spoken, when the thought that I have now to tell you of, flashed across my mind. But, before I say anything more, answer me one question. Am I right in supposing that our attempt at escape must be made in the night?'

'At night, certainly,' says I, 'because we can be most sure, then, that the Pirates off guard are all in this building, and not likely to leave it.'

'I understand. Now, Davis, hear what I have observed of the habits of the men who keep us imprisoned in this place.

The first change of guard at night, is at nine o'clock. At that time, seven men come in from watching, and nine men (the extra night guard) go out to replace them; each party being on duty, as you know, for six hours. I have observed, at the nine o'clock change of guard, that the seven men who come off duty, and the nine who go on, have a supply of baked cakes of Indian corn, reserved expressly for their use. They divide the food between them; the Pirate Captain (who is always astir at the change of guard) generally taking a cake for himself, when the rest of the men take theirs. This makes altogether, seventeen men who partake of food especially reserved for them, at nine o'clock. So far you understand me?'

'Clearly, Miss.'

'The next thing I have noticed, is the manner in which that food is prepared. About two hours before sunset, the Pirate Captain walks out to smoke, after he has eaten the meal which he calls his dinner. In his absence from the hall, the Indians light their fire on the unsheltered side of it, and prepare the last batch of food before they leave us for the night. They knead up two separate masses of dough. The largest is the first which is separated into cakes and baked. That is taken for the use of us prisoners and of the men who are off duty all the night. The second and smaller piece of dough is then pre-pared for the nine o'clock change of guard. On that food – come nearer, Davis, I must say it in a whisper – on that food all our chances of escape now turn. If we can drug it unobserved, the Pirates who go off duty, the Pirates who go on duty, and the Captain, who is more to be feared than all the rest, will be as absolutely insensible to our leaving the Palace, as if they were every one of them dead men.'

I was unable to speak – I was unable even to fetch my breath at those words.

'I have taken Mr Kitten, as a matter of necessity, into our confidence,' she said. 'I have learnt from him a simple way of obtaining the juice of that plant which he forbade the child to eat. I have also made myself acquainted with the quantity which it is necessary to use for our purpose; and I have resolved that no hands but mine shall be charged with the work of kneading it into the dough.'

'Not you, Miss, – not you. Let one of us – let me – run that risk.'

'You have work enough and risk enough already,' said Miss Maryon. 'It is time that the women, for whom you have suffered and ventured so much, should take their share. Besides, the risk is not great, where the Indians only are concerned. They are idle and curious. I have seen, with my own eyes, that they are as easily tempted away from their occupation by any chance sight or chance noise as if they were children; and I have already arranged with Mr Macey that he is to excite their curiosity by suddenly pulling down one of the loose stones in that doorway, when the right time comes. The Indians are certain to run in here to find out what is the matter. Mr Macey will tell them that he has seen a snake, – they will hunt for the creature (as I have seen them hunt, over and over again, in this ruined place) – and while they are so engaged, the opportunity that I want, the two minutes to myself, which are all that I require, will be mine. Dread the Pirate Captain, Davis, for the slightest caprice of his may ruin all our hopes, – but never dread the Indians, and never doubt me.'

Nobody, who had looked in her face at that moment – or at any moment that ever I knew of – could have doubted her.

'There is one thing more,' she went on. 'When is the attempt to be made?'

'In three days' time,' I answered; 'there will be timber enough down to make the rafts.'

'In three days' time, then, let us decide the question of our freedom or our death.' She spoke those words with a firmness that amazed me. 'Rest now,' she said. 'Rest and hope.'

The third day was the hottest we had yet experienced; we were kept longer at work than usual; and when we had done, we left on the bank enough, and more than enough, of timber and poles, to make both the rafts.

The Indians had gone when we got back to the Palace, and the Pirate Captain was still smoking on the flight of steps. As we crossed the hall, I looked on one side and saw the Tortillas set up in a pile, waiting for the men who came in and went out at nine o'clock.

At the door which opened between our room and the women's room, Miss Maryon was waiting for us.

'Is it done?' I asked in a whisper.

'It is done,' she answered.

It was, then, by Mr Macey's watch (which he had kept hidden about him throughout our imprisonment), seven o'clock. We had two hours to wait: hours of suspense, but hours of rest also for the overworked men who had been cutting the wood. Before I lay down, I looked into the inner room. The women were all sitting together; and I saw by the looks they cast on me that Miss Maryon had told them of what was coming with the night. The children were much as usual, playing quiet games among themselves. In the men's room, I noticed that Mr Macey had posted himself along with Tom Packer, close to Serjeant Drooce, and that Mr Fisher seemed to be taking great pains to make himself agreeable to Mr Pordage. I was glad to see that the two gentlemen of the company, who were quick-witted and experienced in most things, were already taking in hand the two unreasonable men.

The evening brought no coolness with it. The heat was so oppressive that we all panted under it. The stillness in the forest was awful. We could almost hear the falling of the leaves.

Half past seven, eight, half past eight, a quarter to nine – Nine. The tramp of feet came up the steps on one side, and the tramp of feet came into the hall, on the other. There was a confusion of voices, – then, the voice of the Pirate Captain, speaking in his own language, – then, the voice of the American mate, ordering out the guard, – then silence.

I crawled to the door of our room, and laid myself down behind it, where I could see a strip of the hall, being that part of it in which the way out was situated. Here, also, the Pirate Captain's tent had been set up, about twelve or fourteen feet from the door. Two torches were burning before it. By their light, I saw the guard on duty file out, each man munching his Tortilla, and each man grumbling over it. At the same time, in the part of the hall which I could not see, I heard the men off duty grumbling also. The Pirate Captain, who had entered his tent the minute before, came out of it, and calling to the American mate, at the far end of the hall, asked sharply in English, what that murmuring meant.

'The men complain of the Tortillas,' the mate tells him. 'They say, they are nastier than ever tonight.'

'Bring me one, and let me taste it,' said the Captain. I had often before heard people talk of their hearts being in their mouths, but I never really knew what the sensation was, till I heard that order given.

The Tortilla was brought to him. He nibbled a bit off it, spat the morsel out with disgust, and threw the rest of the cake away.

'Those Indian beasts have burnt the Tortillas,' he said, 'and their dirty hides shall suffer for it tomorrow morning.' With those words, he whisked round on his heel, and went back into his tent.

Some of the men had crept up behind me, and, looking over my head, had seen what I saw. They passed the account of it in whispers to those who could not see; and they, in their turn, repeated it to the women. In five minutes everybody in the two rooms knew that the scheme had failed with the very man whose sleep it was most important to secure. I heard no stifled crying among the women or stifled cursing among the men. The despair of that time was too deep for tears, and too deep for words.

I myself could not take my eyes off the tent. In a little while he came out of it again, puffing and panting with the heat. He lighted a cigar at one of the torches, and laid himself down on his cloak just inside the doorway leading into the portico, so that all the air from outside might blow over him. Little as he was, he was big enough to lie right across the narrow way out.

He smoked and he smoked, slowly and more slowly, for, what seemed to me to be, hours, but for what, by the watch, was little more than ten minutes after all. Then, the cigar dropped out of his mouth – his hand sought for it, and sank lazily by his side – his head turned over a little towards the door – and he fell off: not into the drugged sleep that there was safety in, but into his light, natural sleep, which a touch on his body might have disturbed.

'Now's the time to gag him,' says Short, creeping up close to me, and taking off his jacket and shoes.

'Steady,' says I. 'Don't let's try that till we can try nothing else. There are men asleep near us who have not eaten the drugged cakes – the Pirate Captain is light and active – and if the gag slips on his mouth, we are all done for. I'll go to his head, Short, with my jacket ready in my hands. When I'm there, do you lead the way with your mates, and step gently into the portico, over his body. Every minute of your time is precious on account of making the rafts. Leave the rest of the men to get the women and children over; and leave me to gag him if he stirs while we are getting out.'

'Shake hands on it, Davis,' says Short, getting to his feet. 'A team of horses wouldn't have dragged me out first, if you hadn't said that about the rafts.'

'Wait a bit,' says I, 'till I speak to Mr Kitten.'

I crawled back into the room, taking care to keep out of the way of the stones in the middle of it, and asked Mr Kitten how long it would be before the drugged cakes acted on the men outside who had eaten them? He said we ought to wait another quarter of an hour, to make quite sure. At the same time, Mr Macey whispered in my ear to let him pass over the Pirate Captain's body, alone with the dangerous man of our company – Serjeant Drooce. 'I know how to deal with mad people,' says he. 'I have persuaded the Serjeant that if he is quiet, and if he steps carefully, I can help him to escape from Tom Packer, whom he is beginning to look on as his keeper.[46] He has been as stealthy and quiet as a cat ever since – and I will answer for him till we get to the riverside.'

What a relief it was to hear that! I was turning round to get back to Short, when a hand touched me lightly.

'I have heard you talking,' whispered Miss Maryon; 'and I will prepare all in my room for the risk we must now run. Robert, the ship's boy, whom the children are so fond of, shall help us to persuade them, once more, that we are going to play a game. If you can get one of the torches from the tent, and pass it in here, it may prevent some of us from stumbling.

85

Don't be afraid of the women and children, Davis. They shall not endanger the brave men who are saving them.'

I left her at once to get the torch. The Pirate Captain was still fast asleep as I stole on tiptoe, into the hall, and took it from the tent. When I returned, and gave it to Miss Maryon, her sister's little deaf-and-dumb boy saw me, and, slipping between us, caught tight hold of one of my hands. Having been used to riding on my shoulders for so many days, he had taken a fancy to me; and, when I tried to put him away, he only clung the tighter, and began to murmur in his helpless dumb way. Slight as the noise was which the poor little fellow could make, we all dreaded it. His mother wrung her hands in despair when she heard him; and Mr Fisher whispered to me for Heaven's sake to quiet the child, and humour him at any cost. I immediately took him up in my arms, and went back to Short.

'Sling him on my back,' says I, 'as you slung the little girl on your own the first day of the march. I want both my hands, and the child won't be quiet away from me.'

Short did as I asked him in two minutes. As soon as he had finished, Mr Macey passed the word on to me, that the quarter of an hour was up; that it was time to try the experiment with Drooce; and that it was necessary for us all to humour him by feigning sleep. We obeyed. Looking out of the corner of my eye, I saw Mr Macey take the mad Serjeant's arm, point round to us all, and then lead him out. Holding tight by Mr Macey, Drooce stepped as lightly as a woman, with as bright and wicked a look of cunning as ever I saw in any human eyes. They crossed the hall – Mr Macey pointed to the Pirate Captain, and whispered, 'Hush!'—the Serjeant imitated the action and repeated the word – then the two stepped over his body (Drooce cautiously raising his feet the highest), and disappeared through the portico. We waited to hear if there was any noise or confusion. Not a sound.

I got up, and Short handed me his jacket for the gag. The child, having been startled from his sleep by the light of the torch, when I brought it in, had fallen off again, already, on my shoulder. 'Now for it,' says I, and stole out into the hall.

I stopped at the tent, went in, and took the first knife I could find there. With the weapon between my teeth, with the little innocent asleep on my shoulder, with the jacket held ready in both hands, I kneeled down on one knee at the Pirate Captain's head, and fixed my eyes steadily on his ugly sleeping face.

The sailors came out first, with their shoes in their hands. No sound of footsteps from any one of them. No movement in the ugly face as they passed over it.

The women and children were ready next. Robert, the ship's boy, lifted the children over: most of them holding their little hands over their mouths to keep from laughing – so well had Robert persuaded them that we were only playing a game. The women passed next, all as light as air; after them, in obedience to a sign from me, my comrades of the Marines, holding their shoes in their hands, as the sailors had done before them. So far, not a word had been spoken, not a mistake had been made – so far, not a change of any sort had passed over the Pirate Captain's face.

There were left now in the hall, besides myself and the child on my back, only Mr Fisher and Mr Pordage. Mr Pordage! Up to that moment, in the risk and excitement of the time, I had not once thought of him.

I was forced to think of him now, though; and with anything but a friendly feeling.

At the sight of the Pirate Captain, asleep across the way out, the unfortunate, mischievous old simpleton tossed up his head, and folded his arms, and was on the point of breaking out loud into a spoken document of some kind, when Mr Fisher wisely and quickly clapped a hand over his mouth.

'Government despatches outside,' whispers Mr Fisher, in an agony. 'Secret service. Forty-nine reports from headquarters, all waiting for you half a mile off. I'll show you the way, sir. Don't wake that man there, who is asleep: he must know nothing about it – he represents the Public.'

Mr Pordage suddenly looked very knowing and hugely satisfied with himself. He followed Mr Fisher to within a foot of the Pirate Captain's body – then stopped short.

'How many reports?' he asked, very anxiously.

'Forty-nine,' said Mr Fisher. 'Come along, sir, – and step clean over the Public, whatever you do.'

Mr Pordage instantly stepped over, as jauntily as if he was going to dance. At the moment of his crossing, a hanging rag of his cursed, useless, unfortunate, limp Diplomatic coat touched the Pirate Captain's forehead, and woke him.

I drew back softly, with the child still asleep on my shoulder, into the black shadow of the wall behind me. At the instant when the Pirate Captain awoke, I had been looking at Mr Pordage, and had consequently lost the chance of applying the gag to his mouth suddenly, at the right time.

On rousing up, he turned his face inwards, towards the prisoners' room. If he had turned it outwards, he must to a dead certainty have seen the tail of Mr Pordage's coat, disappearing in the portico.

Though he was awake enough to move, he was not awake enough to have the full possession of his sharp senses. The drowsiness of his sleep still hung about him. He yawned, stretched himself, spat wearily, sat up, spat again, got on his legs, and stood up, within three feet of the shadow in which I was hiding behind him.

I forgot the knife in my teeth, – I declare solemnly, in the frightful suspense of that moment, I forgot it – and doubled my fist as if I was an unarmed man, with the purpose of stunning him by a blow on the head if he came any nearer. I suppose I waited, with my fist clenched, nearly a minute, while he waited, yawning and spitting. At the end of that time, he made for his tent, and I heard him (with what thankfulness no words can tell!) roll himself down, with another yawn, on his bed inside.

I waited – in the interest of us all – to make quite sure, before I left, that he was asleep again. In what I reckoned as about five minutes' time, I heard him snoring, and felt free to take myself and my little sleeping comrade out of the prison, at last.

The drugged guards in the portico were sitting together, dead asleep, with their backs against the wall. The third man was lying flat, on the landing of the steps. Their arms and ammunition were gone: wisely taken by our men – to defend us, if we were meddled with before we escaped, and to kill food for us when we committed ourselves to the river.

At the bottom of the steps I was startled by seeing two women standing together. They were Mrs Macey and Miss Maryon: the first, waiting to see her child safe; the second (God bless her for it!) waiting to see *me* safe.

In a quarter of an hour we were by the riverside, and saw the work bravely begun: the sailors and the marines under their orders, labouring at the rafts in the shallow water by the bank; Mr Macey and Mr Fisher rolling down fresh timber as it was wanted; the women cutting the vines, creepers, and withies[47] for the lashings. We brought with us three more pair of hands to help; and all worked with such a will, that, in four hours and twenty minutes, by Mr Macey's watch, the rafts, though not finished as they ought to have been, were still strong enough to float us away.

Short, another seaman, and the ship's boy, got aboard the first raft, carrying with them poles and spare timber. Miss Maryon, Mrs Fisher and her husband, Mrs Macey and her husband and three children, Mr and Mrs Pordage, Mr Kitten, myself, and women and children besides, to make up eighteen, were the passengers on the leading raft. The second raft, under the guidance of the two other sailors, held Serjeant Drooce (gagged, for he now threatened to be noisy again), Tom Packer, the two marines, Mrs Belltott, and the rest of the women and children. We all got on board silently and quickly, with a fine moonlight over our heads, and without accidents or delays of any kind.

It was a good half-hour before the time would come for the change of guard at the prison, when the lashings which tied us to the bank were cast off, and we floated away, a company of free people, on the current of an unknown river.

CHAPTER III
THE RAFTS ON THE RIVER
[by Charles Dickens]

We contrived to keep afloat all that night, and, the stream running strong with us, to glide a long way down the river. But, we found the night to be a dangerous time for such navigation, on account of the eddies and rapids, and it was therefore settled next day that in future we would bring-to at sunset, and encamp on the shore. As we knew of no boats that the Pirates possessed, up at the Prison in the Woods, we settled always to encamp on the opposite side of the stream, so as to have the breadth of the river between our sleep and them. Our opinion was, that if they were acquainted with any near way by land to the mouth of this river, they would come up it in force, and retake us or kill us, according as they could; but, that if that was not the case, and if the river ran by none of their secret stations, we might escape.

When I say we settled this or that, I do not mean that we planned anything with any confidence as to what might happen an hour hence. So much had happened in one night, and such great changes had been violently and suddenly made in the fortunes of many among us, that we had got better used to uncertainty, in a little while, than I dare say most people do in the course of their lives.

The difficulties we soon got into, through the off-settings and point-currents[48] of the stream, made the likelihood of our being drowned, alone – to say nothing of our being retaken – as broad and plain as the sun at noonday to all of us. But, we all worked hard at managing the rafts, under the direction of the seamen (of our own skill, I think we never could have prevented them from over-setting), and we also worked hard at making good the defects in their first hasty construction – which the water soon found out. While we humbly resigned ourselves to going down, if it was the will of Our Father that was in Heaven,[49] we humbly made up our minds, that we would all do the best that was in us.

And so we held on, gliding with the stream. It drove us to this bank, and it drove us to that bank, and it turned us, and whirled us; but yet it carried us on. Sometimes much too slowly; sometimes much too fast, but yet it carried us on.

My little deaf-and-dumb boy slumbered a good deal now, and that was the case with all the children. They caused very little trouble to any one. They seemed, in my eyes, to get more like one another, not only in quiet manner, but in the face, too. The motion of the raft was usually so much the same, the scene was usually so much the same, the sound of the soft wash and ripple of the water was usually so much the same, that they were made drowsy, as they might have been by the constant playing of one tune. Even on the grown people, who worked hard and felt anxiety, the same things produced something of the same effect. Every day was so like the other, that I soon lost count of the days, myself, and had to ask Miss Maryon, for instance, whether this was the third or fourth? Miss Maryon had a pocketbook and pencil, and she kept the log; that is to say, she entered up a clear little journal of the time, and of the distances our seamen thought we had made, each night.

So, as I say, we kept afloat and glided on. All day long, and every day, the water, and the woods, and sky; all day long, and every day, the constant watching of both sides of the river, and far ahead at every bold turn and sweep it made, for any signs of Pirate boats, or Pirate dwellings. So, as I say, we kept afloat and glided on. The days melting themselves together to that degree, that I could hardly believe my ears when I asked 'How many, now, Miss?' and she answered, 'Seven.'

To be sure, poor Mr Pordage had, by about now, got his Diplomatic coat into such a state as never was seen. What with the mud of the river, what with the water of the river, what with the sun, and the dews, and the tearing boughs, and the thickets, it hung about him in discoloured shreds like a mop. The sun had touched him a bit. He had taken to always polishing one particular button, which just held on to his left wrist, and to always calling for stationery. I suppose that man called for pens, ink, and paper, tape, and sealing wax, upwards of one thousand times in four and twenty hours. He had an idea that we should never get out of that river unless we were written out of it in a formal Memorandum; and the more we laboured at navigating the rafts, the more he ordered us not to touch them at our peril, and the more he sat and roared for stationery.

Mrs Pordage, similarly, persisted in wearing her nightcap. I doubt if any one but ourselves who had seen the progress of that article of dress, could by this time have told what it was meant for. It had got so limp and ragged that she couldn't see out of her eyes for it. It was so dirty, that whether it was vegetable matter out of a swamp, or weeds out of the river, or an old porter's knot[50] from England, I don't think any new spectator could have said. Yet, this unfortunate old woman had a notion that it was not only vastly genteel, but that it was the correct thing as to propriety. And she really did carry herself over the other ladies who had no nightcaps, and who were forced to tie up their hair how they could, in a superior manner that was perfectly amazing.

I don't know what she looked like, sitting in that blessed nightcap, on a log of wood, outside the hut or cabin upon our raft. She would have rather resembled a fortune-teller in one of the picture books that used to be in the shop windows in my boyhood, except for her stateliness. But, Lord bless my heart, the dignity with which she sat and moped, with her head in that bundle of tatters, was like nothing else in the world! She was not on speaking terms with more than three of the ladies. Some of them had, what she called, 'taken precedence' of her – in getting into, or out of, that miserable little shelter! – and others had not called to pay their respects, or something of that kind. So, there she sat, in her own state and ceremony, while her husband sat on the same log of wood, ordering us one and all to let the raft go to the bottom, and to bring him stationery.

What with this noise on the part of Mr Commissioner Pordage, and what with the cries of Serjeant Drooce on the raft astern (which were sometimes more than Tom Packer could silence), we often made our slow way down the river, anything but quietly. Yet, that it was of great importance that no ears should be able to hear us from the woods on the banks, could not be doubted. We were looked for, to a certainty, and we might be retaken at any moment. It was an anxious time; it was, indeed, indeed, an anxious time.

On the seventh night of our voyage on the rafts, we made fast, as usual, on the opposite side of the river to that from which we had started, in as dark a place as we could pick out. Our little encampment was soon made, and supper was eaten, and the children fell asleep. The watch was set, and everything made orderly for the night. Such a starlight night, with such blue in the sky, and such black in the places of heavy shade on the banks of the great stream!

Those two ladies, Miss Maryon and Mrs Fisher, had always kept near me since the night of the attack. Mr Fisher, who was untiring in the work of our raft, had said to me:

'My dear little childless wife has grown so attached to you, Davis, and you are such a gentle fellow, as well as such a determined one;' our party had adopted that last expression from the one-eyed English pirate, and I repeat what Mr Fisher said, only because he said it; 'that it takes a load off my mind to leave her in your charge.'

I said to him: 'Your lady is in far better charge than mine, Sir, having Miss Maryon to take care of her; but, you may rely upon it, that I will guard them both – faithful and true.'

Says he: 'I do rely upon it, Davis, and I heartily wish all the silver on our old Island was yours.'

That seventh starlight night, as I have said, we made our camp, and got our supper, and set our watch, and the children fell asleep. It was solemn and beautiful in those wild and solitary parts, to see them, every night before they lay down, kneeling under the bright sky, saying their little prayers at women's laps. At that time we men all uncovered, and mostly kept at a distance. When the innocent creatures rose up, we murmured 'Amen!' all together. For, though we had not heard what they said, we knew it must be good for us.

At that time, too, as was only natural, those poor mothers in our company whose children had been killed, shed many tears. I thought the sight seemed to console them while it made them cry; but, whether I was right or wrong in that, they wept very much. On this seventh night, Mrs Fisher had cried for her lost darling until she cried herself asleep. She was lying on a little couch of leaves and such-like (I made the best little couch I could, for them every night), and Miss Maryon had covered her, and sat by her, holding her hand. The stars looked down upon them. As for me, I guarded them.

'Davis!' says Miss Maryon. (I am not going to say what a voice she had. I couldn't if I tried.)

'I am here, Miss.'

'The river sounds as if it were swollen tonight.'

'We all think, Miss, that we are coming near the sea.'

'Do you believe, now, we shall escape?'

'I do now, Miss, really believe it.' I had always said I did; but, I had in my own mind been doubtful.

'How glad you will be, my good Davis, to see England again!'

I have another confession to make that will appear singular. When she said these words, something rose in my throat; and the stars I looked away at, seemed to break into sparkles that fell down my face and burnt it.

'England is not much to me, Miss, except as a name.'

'Oh! So true an Englishman should not say that! – Are you not well tonight, Davis?' Very kindly, and with a quick change.

'Quite well, Miss.'

'Are you sure? Your voice sounds altered in my hearing.'

'No, Miss, I am a stronger man than ever. But, England is nothing to me.'

Miss Maryon sat silent for so long a while, that I believed she had done speaking to me for one time. However, she had not; for by and by she said in a distinct, clear tone:

'No, good friend; you must not say, that England is nothing to you. It is to be much to you, yet – everything to you. You have to take back to England the good name you have earned here, and the gratitude and attachment and respect you have won here; and you have to make some good English girl very happy and proud, by marrying her; and I shall one day see her, I hope, and make her happier and prouder still, by telling her what noble services her husband's were in South America, and what a noble friend he was to me there.'

Though she spoke these kind words in a cheering manner, she spoke them compassionately. I said nothing. It will appear to be another strange confession, that I paced to and fro, within call, all that night, a most unhappy man reproaching myself all the night long. 'You are as ignorant as any man alive; you are as obscure as any man alive; you are as poor as any man alive; you are no better than the mud under your foot.' That was the way in which I went on against myself until the morning.

With the day, came the day's labour. What I should have done without the labour, I don't know. We were afloat again at the usual hour, and were again making our way down the river. It was broader, and clearer of obstructions than it had been, and it seemed to flow faster. This was one of Drooce's quiet days; Mr Pordage, besides being sulky, had almost lost his voice; and we made good way, and with little noise.

There was always a seaman forward on the raft, keeping a bright lookout. Suddenly, in the full heat of the day, when the children were slumbering, and the very trees and reeds appeared to be slumbering, this man – it was Short – holds up his hand, and cries with great caution:

'Avast! Voices ahead!'

We held on against the stream as soon as we could bring her up, and the other raft followed suit. At first, Mr Macey, Mr Fisher, and myself, could hear nothing; though both the seamen aboard of us agreed that they could hear voices and oars. After a little pause, however, we united in thinking that we *could* hear the sound of voices, and the dip of oars. But, you can hear a long way in those countries, and there was a bend of the river before us, and nothing was to be seen except such waters and such banks as we were now in the eighth day (and might, for the matter of our feelings, have been in the eightieth), of having seen with anxious eyes.

It was soon decided to put a man ashore who should creep through the wood, see what was coming, and warn the rafts. The rafts in the meantime to keep the middle of the stream. The man to be put ashore, and not to swim ashore, as the first thing could be more quickly done than the second. The raft conveying him, to get back into midstream, and to hold on along with the other, as well as it could, until signalled by the man. In case of danger, the man to shift for himself until it should be safe to take him aboard again. I volunteered to be the man.

We knew that the voices and oars must come up slowly against the stream; and our seamen knew, by the set of the stream, under which bank they would come. I was put ashore accordingly. The raft got off well, and I broke into the wood.

Steaming hot it was, and a tearing place to get through. So much the better for me, since it was something to contend against and do. I cut off the bend in the river, at a great saving of space, came to the water's edge again, and hid myself, and waited. I could now hear the dip of the oars very distinctly; the voices had ceased.

The sound came on in a regular tune, and as I lay hidden, I fancied the tune so played to be, 'Chris'en – George – King! Chris'en – George – King! Chris'en – George – King!' over and over again, always the same, with the pauses always at the same places. I had likewise time to make up my mind that if these were the Pirates, I could and would (barring my being shot), swim off to my raft, in spite of my wound, the moment I had given the alarm, and hold my old post by Miss Maryon.

'Chris'en – George – King! Chris'en – George – King! Chris'en – George – King!'coming up, now, very near.

I took a look at the branches about me, to see where a shower of bullets would be most likely to do me least hurt; and

I took a look back at the track I had made in forcing my way in; and now I was wholly prepared and fully ready for them.

'Chris'en – George – King! Chris'en – George – King! Chris'en – George – King!' Here they were!

Who were they? The barbarous Pirates, scum of all nations, headed by such men as the hideous little Portuguese monkey, and the one-eyed English convict with the gash across his face, that ought to have gashed his wicked head off? The worst men in the world picked out from the worst, to do the cruellest and most atrocious deeds that ever stained it? The howling, murdering, black-flag waving, mad, and drunken crowd of devils that had overcome us by numbers and by treachery? No. These were English men in English boats – good bluejackets and redcoats – marines that I knew myself, and sailors that knew our seamen! At the helm of the first boat, Captain Carton, eager and steady. At the helm of the second boat, Captain Maryon, brave and bold. At the helm of the third boat, an old seaman, with determination carved into his watchful face, like the figurehead of a ship. Every man doubly and trebly armed from head to foot. Every man lying-to at his work, with a will that had all his heart and soul in it. Every man looking out for any trace of friend or enemy, and burning to be the first to do good, or avenge evil. Every man with his face on fire when he saw me, his countryman who had been taken prisoner, and hailed me with a cheer, as Captain Carton's boat ran in and took me on board.

I reported, 'All escaped, sir! All well, all safe, all here!'

God bless me – and God bless them – what a cheer! It turned me weak, as I was passed on from hand to hand to the stern of the boat: every hand patting me or grasping me in some way or other, in the moment of my going by.

'Hold up, my brave fellow,' says Captain Carton, clapping me on the shoulder like a friend, and giving me a flask. 'Put your lips to that, and they'll be red again. Now, boys, give way!'

The banks flew by us, as if the mightiest stream that ever ran was with us; and so it was, I am sure, meaning the stream of those men's ardour and spirit. The banks flew by us, and we came in sight of the rafts – the banks flew by us, and we came alongside of the rafts – the banks stopped; and there was a tumult of laughing and crying and kissing and shaking of hands, and catching up of children and setting of them down again, and a wild hurry of thankfulness and joy that melted every one and softened all hearts.

I had taken notice, in Captain Carton's boat, that there was a curious and quite new sort of fitting on board. It was a kind of a little bower made of flowers, and it was set up behind the captain, and betwixt him and the rudder. Not only was this arbor, so to call it, neatly made of flowers, but it was ornamented in a singular way. Some of the men had taken the ribbons and buckles off their hats, and hung them among the flowers; others, had made festoons and streamers of their handkerchiefs, and hung them there; others, had intermixed such trifles as bits of glass and shining fragments of lockets and tobacco boxes, with the flowers; so that altogether it was a very bright and lively object in the sunshine. But, why there, or what for, I did not understand.

Now, as soon as the first bewilderment was over, Captain Carton gave the order to land for the present. But, this boat of his, with two hands left in her, immediately put off again when the men were out of her, and kept off, some yards from the shore. As she floated there, with the two hands gently backing water to keep her from going down the stream, this pretty little arbor attracted many eyes. None of the boat's crew, however, had anything to say about it, except that it was the captain's fancy.

The captain, with the women and children clustering round him, and the men of all ranks grouped outside them, and all listening, stood telling how the Expedition, deceived by its bad intelligence, had chased the light Pirate boats all that fatal night, and had still followed in their wake next day, and had never suspected until many hours too late that the great Pirate body had drawn off in the darkness when the chace began, and shot over to the Island. He stood telling how the Expedition, supposing the whole array of armed boats to be ahead of it, got tempted into shallows and went aground; but, not without having its revenge upon the two decoy boats, both of which it had come up with, overland, and sent to the bottom with all on board. He stood telling how the Expedition, fearing then that the case stood as it did, got afloat again, by great exertion, after the loss of four more tides, and returned to the Island, where they found the sloop scuttled and the treasure gone. He stood telling how my officer, Lieutenant Linderwood, was left upon the Island, with as strong a force as could be got together hurriedly from the mainland, and how the three boats we saw before us were manned and armed and had come away, exploring the coast and inlets, in search of any tidings of us. He stood telling all this, with his face to the river; and, as he stood telling it, the little arbor of flowers floated in the sunshine before all the faces there.

Leaning on Captain Carton's shoulder, between him and Miss Maryon, was Mrs Fisher, her head drooping on her arm. She asked him, without raising it, when he had told so much, whether he had found her mother?

'Be comforted! She lies,' said the Captain, gently, 'under the coconut trees on the beach.'

'And my child, Captain Carton, did you find my child, too? Does my darling rest with my mother?'

'No. Your pretty child sleeps,' said the Captain, 'under a shade of flowers.'

His voice shook; but, there was something in it that struck all the hearers. At that moment, there sprung from the arbor in his boat, a little creature, clapping her hands and stretching out her arms, and crying, 'Dear papa! Dear mamma! I am not killed. I am saved. I am coming to kiss you. Take me to them, take me to them, good, kind sailors!'

Nobody who saw that scene has ever forgotten it, I am sure, or ever will forget it. The child had kept quite still, where her brave grandmama had put her (first whispering in her ear, 'Whatever happens to me, do not stir, my dear!'), and had remained quiet until the fort was deserted; she had then crept out of the trench, and gone into her mother's house; and there, alone on the solitary Island, in her mother's room, and asleep on her mother's bed, the Captain had found her. Nothing could induce her to be parted from him after he took her up in his arms, and he had brought her away with him, and the men had made the bower for her. To see those men now, was a sight. The joy of the women was beautiful; the joy of those women who had lost their own children, was quite sacred and divine; but, the ecstasies of Captain Carton's boat's crew, when their pet was restored to her parents, were wonderful for the tenderness they showed in the midst of roughness. As the Captain stood with the child in his arms, and the child's own little arms now clinging round his neck, now round her father's, now round her mother's, now round someone who pressed up to kiss her, the boat's crew shook hands with one another, waved their hats over their heads, laughed, sang, cried, danced – and all among themselves, without wanting to interfere with anybody – in a manner never to be represented. At last, I saw the coxswain and another, two very hard-faced men with grizzled heads who had been the heartiest of the hearty all along, close with one another, get each of them the other's head under his arm, and pummel away at it with his fist as hard as he could, in his excess of joy.

When we had well rested and refreshed ourselves – and very glad we were to have some of the heartening things to eat and drink that had come up in the boats – we recommenced our voyage down the river: rafts, and boats, and all. I said to myself, it was a very different kind of voyage now, from what it had been; and I fell into my proper place and station among my fellow soldiers.

But, when we halted for the night, I found that Miss Maryon had spoken to Captain Carton concerning me. For, the Captain came straight up to me, and says he, 'My brave fellow, you have been Miss Maryon's bodyguard all along, and you shall remain so. Nobody shall supersede you in the distinction and pleasure of protecting that young lady.' I thanked his honour in the fittest words I could find, and that night I was placed on my old post of watching the place where she slept. More than once in the night, I saw Captain Carton come out into the air, and stroll about there, to see that all was well. I have now this other singular confession to make, that I saw him with a heavy heart. Yes; I saw him with a heavy, heavy heart.

In the daytime, I had the like post in Captain Carton's boat. I had a special station of my own, behind Miss Maryon, and no hands but hers ever touched my wound. (It has been healed these many long years; but, no other hands have ever touched it.) Mr Pordage was kept tolerably quiet now, with pen and ink, and began to pick up his senses a little. Seated in the second boat, he made documents with Mr Kitten, pretty well all day; and he generally handed in a Protest about something whenever we stopped. The Captain, however, made so very light of these papers that it grew into a saying among the men, when one of them wanted a match for his pipe, 'Hand us over a Protest, Jack!' As to Mrs Pordage, she still wore the nightcap, and she now had cut all the ladies on account of her not having been formally and separately rescued by Captain Carton before anybody else. The end of Mr Pordage, to bring to an end all I know about him, was, that he got great compliments at home for his conduct on these trying occasions, and that he died of yellow jaundice, a Governor and a K.C.B.[51]

Serjeant Drooce had fallen from a high fever into a low one, Tom Packer – the only man who could have pulled the Serjeant through it – kept hospital aboard the old raft, and Mrs Belltott, as brisk as ever again (but the spirit of that little woman, when things tried it, was not equal to appearances), was head-nurse under his directions. Before we got down to the Mosquito coast, the joke had been made by one of our men, that we should see her gazetted Mrs Tom Packer, *vice* Belltott exchanged.[52]

When we reached the coast, we got native boats as sub-stitutes for the rafts; and we rowed along under the land; and in that beautiful climate, and upon that beautiful water, the blooming days were like enchantment. Ah! They were running away, faster than any sea or river, and there was no tide to bring them back. We were coming very near the settlement where the people of Silver-Store were to be left, and from which we Marines were under orders to return to Belize.

Captain Carton had, in the boat by him, a curious long-barreled Spanish gun, and he had said to Miss Maryon one day that it was the best of guns, and had turned his head to me, and said:

'Gill Davis, load her fresh with a couple of slugs, against a chance of showing how good she is.'

So, I had discharged the gun over the sea, and had loaded her, according to orders, and there it had lain at the Captain's feet, convenient to the Captain's hand.

The last day but one of our journey was an uncommonly hot day. We started very early; but, there was no cool air on the sea as the day got on, and by noon the heat was really hard to bear, considering that there were women and children to bear it. Now, we happened to open, just at that time, a very pleasant little cove or bay, where there was a deep shade from a great growth of trees. Now, the Captain, therefore, made the signal to the other boats to follow him in and lie by a while.

The men who were off duty went ashore, and lay down, but were ordered, for caution's sake, not to stray, and to keep within view. The others rested on their oars, and dozed. Awnings had been made of one thing and another, in all the boats, and the passengers found it cooler to be under them in the shade, when there was room enough, than to be in the thick woods. So, the passengers were all afloat, and mostly sleeping. I kept my post behind Miss Maryon, and she was on Captain Carton's right in the boat, and Mrs Fisher sat on her right again. The Captain had Mrs Fisher's daughter on his knee. He and the two ladies were talking about the Pirates, and were talking softly: partly, because people do talk softly under such indolent circumstances, and partly because the little girl had gone off asleep.

I think I have before given it out for my Lady to write down, that Captain Carton had a fine bright eye of his own. All at once, he darted me a side look, as much as to say. 'Steady–don't take on – I see something!' – and gave the child into her mother's arms. That eye of his was so easy to understand, that

I obeyed it by not so much as looking either to the right or to the left out of a corner of my own, or changing my attitude the least trifle. The Captain went on talking in the same mild and easy way; but began – with his arms resting across his knees, and his head a little hanging forward, as if the heat were rather too much for him – began to play with the Spanish gun.

'They had laid their plans, you see,' says the Captain, taking up the Spanish gun across his knees, and looking, lazily, at the inlaying on the stock, 'with a great deal of art; and the corrupt or blundering local authorities were so easily deceived;' he ran his left hand idly along the barrel, but I saw, with my breath held, that he covered the action of cocking the gun with his right – 'so easily deceived, that they summoned us out to come into the trap. But my intention as to future operations – ' In a flash the Spanish gun was at his bright eye, and he fired.

All started up; innumerable echoes repeated the sound of the discharge; a cloud of bright-colored birds flew out of the woods screaming; a handful of leaves were scattered in the place where the shot had struck; a crackling of branches was heard; and some lithe but heavy creature sprang into the air, and fell forward, head down, over the muddy bank.

'What is it?' cries Captain Maryon from his boat. All silent then, but the echoes rolling away.

'It is a Traitor and a Spy,' said Captain Carton, handing me the gun to load again. 'And I think the other name of the animal is Christian George King!'

Shot through the heart. Some of the people ran round to the spot, and drew him out, with the slime and wet trickling down his face; but, his face itself would never stir any more to the end of time.

'Leave him hanging to that tree,' cried Captain Carton; his boat's crew giving way, and he leaping ashore. 'But first into this wood, every man in his place. And boats! Out of gunshot!'

It was a quick change, well meant and well made, though it ended in disappointment. No Pirates were there; no one but the Spy was found. It was supposed that the Pirates, unable to retake us, and expecting a great attack upon them, to be the consequence of our escape, had made from the ruins in the Forest, taken to their ship along with the Treasure, and left the Spy to pick up what intelligence he could. In the evening we went away, and he was left hanging to the tree, all alone, with the red sun making a kind of a dead sunset on his black face.

Next day, we gained the settlement on the Mosquito coast for which we were bound. Having stayed there to refresh, seven days, and having been much commended, and highly spoken of, and finely entertained, we Marines stood under orders to march from the town gate (it was neither much of a town nor much of a gate), at five in the morning.

My officer had joined us before then. When we turned out at the gate, all the people were there; in the front of them all those who had been our fellow prisoners, and all the seamen.

'Davis,' says Lieutenant Linderwood. 'Stand out, my friend!'

I stood out from the ranks, and Miss Maryon and Captain Carton came up to me.

'Dear Davis,' says Miss Maryon, while the tears fell fast down her face, 'your grateful friends, in most unwillingly taking leave of you, ask the favour that, while you bear away with you their affectionate remembrance which nothing can ever impair, you will also take this purse of money – far more valuable to you, we all know, for the deep attachment and thankfulness with which it is offered, than for its own contents, though we hope those may prove useful to you, too, in after life.'

I got out, in answer, that I thankfully accepted the attachment and affection, but not the money. Captain Carton looked at me very attentively, and stepped back, and moved away. I made him my bow as he stepped back, to thank him for being so delicate.

'No, miss,' said I, 'I think it would break my heart to accept of money. But, if you could condescend to give to a man so ignorant and common as myself, any little thing you have worn – such as a bit of ribbon –'

She took a ring from her finger, and put it in my hand. And she rested her hand in mine, while she said these words:

'The brave gentlemen of old – but not one of them was braver, or had a nobler nature than you – took such gifts from ladies, and did all their good actions for the givers' sakes. If you will do yours for mine, I shall think with pride that I continue to have some share in the life of a gallant and generous man.'

For the second time in my life, she kissed my hand. I made so bold, for the first time, as to kiss hers; and I tied the ring at my breast, and I fell back to my place.

Then, the horse-litter went out at the gate, with Serjeant Drooce in it; and the horse-litter went out at the gate with Mrs Belltott in it; and Lieutenant Linderwood gave the word of command, 'Quick march!' and, cheered and cried for, we went out of the gate too, marching along the level plain towards the serene blue sky as if we were marching straight to Heaven.

When I have added here that the Pirate scheme was blown to shivers, by the Pirate ship which had the Treasure on board being so vigorously attacked by one of His Majesty's cruisers, among the West India Keys, and being so swiftly boarded and carried, that nobody suspected anything about the scheme until three-fourths of the Pirates were killed, and the other fourth were in irons, and the Treasure was recovered; I come to the last singular confession I have got to make.

It is this. I well knew what an immense and hopeless distance there was between me and Miss Maryon; I well knew that I was no fitter company for her than I was for the angels; I well knew that she was as high above my reach as the sky over my head; and yet I loved her. What put it in my low heart to be so daring, or whether such a thing ever happened before or since, as that a man so uninstructed and obscure as myself got his unhappy thoughts lifted up to such a height, while knowing very well how presumptuous and impossible to be realised they were, I am unable to say; still, the suffering to me was just as great as if I had been a gentleman. I suffered agony – agony. I suffered hard, and I suffered long. I thought of her last words to me, however, and I never disgraced them. If it had not been for those dear words, I think I should have lost myself in despair and recklessness.

The ring will be found lying on my heart, of course, and will be laid with me wherever I am laid. I am getting on in years now, though I am able and hearty. I was recommended for promotion, and everything was done to reward me that could be done; but, my total want of all learning stood in my way, and I found myself so completely out of the road to it, that I could not conquer any learning, though I tried. I was long in the service, and I respected it, and was respected in it, and the service is dear to me at this present hour.

At this present hour, when I give this out to my Lady to be written down, all my old pain has softened away, and I am as happy as a man can be, at this present fine old country house of Admiral Sir George Carton, Baronet. It was my Lady Carton who herself sought me out, over a great many miles of the wide world, and found me in Hospital wounded, and brought me here. It is my Lady Carton who writes down my words. My Lady was Miss Maryon. And now, that I conclude what I had to tell, I see my Lady's honoured grey hair droop over her face, as she leans a little lower at her desk; and I fervently thank her for being so tender as I see she is, towards the past pain and trouble of her poor, old, faithful, humble soldier.

THE END OF THE
CHRISTMAS NUMBER FOR 1857.

NOTES

1. Lucas, Samuel. 'Charles Dickens's Christmas Story', *The Times* 24th December 1857, p. 4.

2. *The Pilgrim Edition of the Letters of Charles Dickens*, vol. 8, p. 469, Oxford 1995.

3. *The Pilgrim Edition of the Letters of Charles Dickens*, vol. 8, p. 459, Oxford 1995.

4. *The Pilgrim Edition of the Letters of Charles Dickens*, vol. 8, pp. 507–08, Oxford 1995.

5. Often, Victorians signed letters with 'Yours to command', and Gill Davis begins rather than ends his narrative with the phrase to assert the text's authenticity. As readers soon learn, Gill cannot read or write, which is why he references his signature (presumably appearing on the fictional manuscript) as his 'Mark': an 'x' or a cross.

6. Bulwarks are elevated pieces of woodwork that surround a vessel and serve a protective function; with a single mast, a sloop is a small, armed ship. Stretching across the eastern (Caribbean) coast of present-day Nicaragua and Honduras, the borders of what is referred to as the Mosquito Coast shifted throughout history. In this region, the British sometimes colonized (as in the case of Belize), fought the Spanish in an attempt to take over lands, or formed alliances with indigenous peoples to oppose the Spanish (setting up a British 'protectorate').

7. According to Gadd and Phillip, the location described by Gill Davis corresponds to Snolledge Bottom, a valley to the east of Chatham-Maidstone Road in Kent that is also home to Snodhurst Farm (*A Dickens Dictionary*). Dickens purchased Gad's Hill Place in Higham, Kent in 1856 and took long walks in the region; his friend and biographer John Forster quotes a letter in which Dickens proclaims, just before writing *The Perils*, 'I have discovered that the seven miles between Maidstone and Rochester is one of the most beautiful walks in England' (see *The Pilgrim Edition of the Letters of Charles Dickens*, vol. 8, p. 455, Oxford 1995).

8. A light-hearted but nevertheless sharp critique of the rote performance of Christian rituals by parish officials, such as the Beadle (a figure also notably featured in Dickens' *Oliver Twist*). 'The Catechism' in *The Book of Common Prayer* (1662 edition) instructs: 'Quest. Who gave you this Name? Answ. My Godfathers and Godmothers in my Baptism; wherein I was made a member of Christ, the child of God, and an inheritor of the kingdom of heaven.'

9. Dickens would use 'all the year round' as the title for the journal he launched on 30th April 1859 to replace *Household Words*, a publication he discontinued as the result of a disagreement with the publishers Bradbury and Evans after they refused to print in *Punch* a scandalous 'Personal Statement' Dickens wrote about his marital affairs. (The statement did appear on 7th June 1858 in *The Times* of London and was later reprinted in *Household Words* and *The New York Times*).

10. An officer serving as quartermaster would perform a range of duties, including compass reading; signal sending and receiving; and the management of camp logistics, presumably with clear penmanship necessary for supply records and other communications.

11. In 1655, Britain defeated Spain and took control of the island of Jamaica. Heavily dependent on human slave labour, the colony's main export was sugar. Jamaica gained independence in 1962 and remains a member of the Commonwealth of Nations. Present-day Belize officially became a British colony in 1862 and was known as British Honduras. Historically a heavily disputed area, with indigenous people, Britain, Spain, Guatemala and Mexico fighting for control, Belize gained independence in 1981 and remains a member of the Commonwealth of Nations.

12. Wealthy citizens and noblemen could purchase commissions granting them instant officer status and command over troops, while non-commissioned soldiers rose through the ranks to become officers but were never granted equivalent authority. This much-criticized system, which Dickens abhorred and which insured that the wealthy classes ruled the military, had been in place since the seventeenth century and lasted to 1871.

13. Sambo is a derogatory term for persons of African descent, especially those in positions regarded as subservient, and is often but not exclusively used to refer to people with shared African and Indian, South American or European ancestry.

14. As no official 'South American flag' existed in 1744, this is likely a reference to the British flag flying alongside the Burgundy Cross Flag (of the Viceroyalty of New Spain whose holdings in the area were vast), indicating an agreement between the two countries in regard to exports and shared occupancy.

15. Another island under British control in the Caribbean; excepting a period of French rule from 1779–83, the British held St Vincent from 1762–1979.

16. Sangaree, or sangria, was originally regarded in the eighteenth century as a sort of wine punch made from red wine mixed with spices, such as nutmeg, fruit and sugar. Nineteenth-century recipes include watered-down ale or porter as the alcohol base.

17. In addition to Snorridge Bottom, the name Pordage appears in the area of Dickens' childhood and later residence. In *The Childhood and Youth of Charles Dickens*, Robert Langton describes gravestones next to Rochester Cathedral bearing the names of a Caleb Pordage as well as a Fanny Dorrett (Dickens finished his novel *Little Dorrit* just before writing this number). The model for Pordage was Lord Canning, Governor-General of India, with whose policies in regard to the Indian Rebellion Dickens disagreed.

18. 29th September is Michaelmas Day, in honour of Saint Michael and often celebrated with goose and special cake. Michaelmas was a quarter day when rents came due and marked the end of harvest season.

19. 'Native' oysters are harvested from British waters, even if from an artificially created bed.

20. Sailors with permission to remain ashore.

21. The rear of the vessel, usually providing seating for its commander or passengers.

22. Covered in black lacquer or varnish (as opposed to folding 'japanned' screens featuring calligraphy and elaborate decorative painting).

23. A non-commissioned officer who attends the Captain and commands the vessel unless or until a higher-ranking officer takes over.

24. The legendary Saint George cowed a pestilence-breathing dragon to save a sacrificed maiden. After rescuing the girl, he promised to kill the dragon if the frightened residents converted to Christianity; they converted, and Saint George beheaded the beast.

25. Rullocks, or rowlocks, are devices that hold the oars of a boat in place along the gunwale, or upper edge, of the vessel, where oars knocking about could be quite noisy.

26. A black flag identified pirates and became known as the 'Jolly Roger', an anglicized version of *joli rouge,* which describes the original red colour of the pirate flag. Red warned that, without immediate surrender, the pirates would kill rather than imprison all fighters, and red pirate flags remained common even after black flags increased in the early 1700s. Also see Note 40 below.

27. Pordage's direction to 'treat the enemy with great delicacy, consideration, clemency, and forbearance' is a satiric representation of Lord Canning's policy of discriminating between sepoys who were involved directly in the Indian Rebellion and sepoys who were enlisted in other regiments and thus not deserving of violent retribution. Carton's speech nearly matches Dickens' articulation of his own feelings in a letter to Emile de la Rue from 23rd October 1857, 'I wish I were Commander in Chief over there! I would address that Oriental character which must be powerfully spoken to, in something like the following placard, which should be vigorously translated into all native dialects, "I, the Inimitable, holding this office of mine, and firmly believing that I Hold it by the permission of Heaven and not by the appointment of Satan, have the honour to inform you Hindoo gentry that it is my intention, with all possible avoidance of unnecessary cruelty and with all merciful swiftness of execution, to exterminate the Race from the face of the earth, which disfigured the earth with the late abominable atrocities"'(*The Pilgrim Letters*, Vol 8, p. 473, Oxford 1995).

28. The Maltese gained a reputation as pirates in part because the Knights of St John, quartered on the island of Malta from 1530–1798, regularly attacked, plundered, and enslaved the crews of ships from the North African Barbary coast that were attempting to traverse the central Mediterranean Sea.

29. Here, 'double-dyed' does not suggest conflicted allegiances but rather that the traitor is so thoroughly soaked in corruption as to be doubly stained by it (language which resonates strongly with the racist labeling of Christian George King as a black 'sambo').

30. Giving Gill a 'breather' here means that Drooce has fought intensely enough to take away Gill's breath (rather than giving Gill a 'breather', or rest, to catch his breath).

31. A sword with a short, flat blade used primarily in hand-to-hand combat between sailors.

32. Drooce is calling the pirates pests, as a cockchafer is a large, destructive beetle also known as a Maybug or May beetle because of the time of year when it emerges.

33. Shrivelled or wrinkled.

34. Dandies wore brightly colored, fashionable clothing and were keen to be seen in the area of Pall Mall, which housed gentleman's clubs in London's West End. Collins and Dickens shared a taste for extravagant, sometimes flashy styles of dress.

35. Initially a name for an energetic adolescent bull, the term 'bullock' expanded to describe particularly vigorous young men.

36. Originally a fine, close weave of French linen, in the nineteenth-century cambric increasingly referred to a similar weave of thin cotton, usually white.

37. A crooked or curved pen-stroke, resembling a hook used for hanging pots near cooking fires or for lifting pot lids.

38. Pieces of chewing tobacco.

39. Grog is sugared and diluted rum named for 'Old Grog', Admiral Edward Vernon (1684–1757), whose nickname stemmed from his cloak's grogram material (usually a coarse blend of wool and silk). In 1740, Admiral Vernon changed sailors' daily ration from brandy to grog in an attempt to curb drunkenness.

40. Captains recorded deaths in ships' logs with a skull, which pirates appropriated to represent their murderous intent. The first recorded reference to the skull and crossbones pirate flag is from the year 1700 and reports that Emanuel Wynne, a French pirate, flew the flag with the inclusion of an hourglass image.

41. This region is home to several varieties of brightly-coloured Amazonian parrot species, including parakeets and macaws. Two of the most commonly sighted are the white-crowned parrot and the Tovi parakeet (or orange-chinned parakeet).

42. These would be Platyrrhini, or 'New World' monkeys with flat, broad noses as opposed to Catarrhini or 'Old World' monkeys with narrower, higher-sloping noses. There are at least ninety-four species of Platyrrhini monkeys in Central and South America, including marmosets and spider monkeys.

43. The description of ruins in this region evokes the Mayan Indians and the architecture for which they are known. Two sites of such jungle ruins in the area are Tikal and Uaxactun in present-day Guatemala.

44. On three sides, the earth and rocks have been mounded and formed into steep, sloping walls.

45. The most forward section of a ship, around the foremast, where sailors' quarters were often located.

46. The original text, with what appears to be a printer's error, reads 'whom he is beginning look on as his keeper'.

47. Pliable sticks or branches, often willows.

48. Off-settings can refer to multiple hazards here, including the wooden rafts being turned sideways by various upwellings or downwellings; point-currents come from the direction in which the rafts are heading.

49. See Matthew 6:7–9, in which Jesus discourages praying with too 'many words' and instructs instead, 'Pray then like this:/Our Father who art in heaven,/Hallowed be thy name'.

50. To assist with the carrying of heavy parcels or loads, a porter's knot consisted mainly of pads for the shoulders, sometimes connected to a loop of fabric that would lay flat against the forehead to help distribute the weight more evenly.

51. Ranking under a Knight Grand Cross, a Knight Commander of the Bath receives the honour in commemoration of civilian or military service. The Most Honourable Order of the Bath, established in 1725 by King George I, takes its name from purifying bathing rituals, and its badge hangs on a red ribbon.

52. Announced as his wife in an official government journal, or gazette.

Wilkie Collins (1824–89) was an innovator in the genres of detective and sensation fiction and was one of Dickens' closest companions and collaborators. The two writers frequently travelled to Europe together, collaborated on numerous pieces of short fiction, and jointly staged theatrical productions, including *The Frozen Deep* (1857). Collins wrote for both of Dickens' journals, *Household Words* and *All the Year Round*, contributing to many of the annual Christmas numbers. Some of Collins' most successful novels, including the phenomenally popular *The Woman in White* (1860) and *The Moonstone* (1868), appeared serially in *All the Year Round*, which he sometimes managed in Dickens' absence. In addition to his work as a novelist and playwright, Collins found success as a journalist for several periodicals and wrote a well-received travel book, *Rambles Beyond Railways* (1851). Collins' best known work, *The Moonstone*, is one of the first detective novels in the English language and remains one of the most impressive examples of the form. His fiction often challenged nineteenth-century social convention, giving voice to characters with physical disabilities and advocating a subversion of sexual norms. In Collins' personal life, he raised children with two women simultaneously, maintaining each in her own household and consistently opposing the institution of marriage.

Charles Dickens (1812–70), a true celebrity in the Victorian period, remains one of the best-known British writers. His most popular works, such as *A Christmas Carol* (1843) and *Great Expectations* (1861), continue to be read and adapted worldwide. In addition to fourteen complete novels, Dickens wrote short stories, essays, and plays. He acted on the stage more than once in amateur theatricals of his own production, and at the end of his life gave a series of powerful public readings from his works. Dickens' journalism is a lesser-known yet central aspect of his life and career. In 1850, he founded *Household Words*, where he worked as editor in chief in addition to writing over one hundred pieces himself. A dispute with his publishers, one of whom was representing his wife Catherine in negotiations over their marital separation, caused Dickens to fold *Household Words* into a new journal, *All the Year Round*, in 1859. From 1850–67, Dickens published a special issue of these journals each December that he called the Christmas number. Collaborative in nature, including the work of up to nine different authors, the Christmas numbers were extremely popular and frequently imitated by other publishers. *The Perils of Certain English Prisoners* is the first Christmas number to include only one author other than Dickens, and its popularity spawned multiple theatrical adaptations.

Melisa Klimaszewski is an Associate Professor at Drake University, where she specialises in Victorian literature, critical race and gender studies, and the literature of South Africa. She is author of *Wilkie Collins* in Hesperus' *Brief Lives* series, and she has edited several of Dickens' collaborative Christmas numbers, including *A Round of Stories by the Christmas Fire*, *The Holly-Tree Inn*, and *The Seven Poor Travellers*. With Melissa Valiska Gregory, she is co-author of *Charles Dickens* in the *Brief Lives* series and co-editor of *The Lazy Tour of Two Idle Apprentices*, *The Wreck of the Golden Mary*, *Somebody's Luggage*, and *Doctor Marigold's Prescriptions*.

HESPERUS PRESS

Hesperus Press is committed to bringing near what is far – far both in space and time. Works written by the greatest authors, and unjustly neglected or simply little known in the English-speaking world, are made accessible through new translations and a completely fresh editorial approach. Through these classic works, the reader is introduced to the greatest writers from all times and all cultures.

For more information on Hesperus Press, please visit our website: **www.hesperuspress.com**